Murder in Crystal

A Savannah Williams Mystery

Debi Chestnut

Copyright © 2004 by Debra Chestnut

All rights reserved. No part of this book shall be reproduced or transmitted in any form or by any means, electronic, mechanical, magnetic, photographic including photocopying, recording or by any information storage and retrieval system, without prior written permission of the publisher. No patent liability is assumed with respect to the use of the information contained herein. Although every precaution has been taken in the preparation of this book, the publisher and author assume no responsibility for errors or omissions. Neither is any liability assumed for damages resulting from the use of the information contained herein.

This is a work of fiction. Names, characters, places, and incidents either are the product of the author's imagination or are used fictitiously. Any resemblance to actual events or locales or persons, living or dead, is entirely coincidental.

ISBN 0-7414-2091-0

Published by:

1094 New Dehaven Street, Suite 100
West Conshohocken, PA 19428-2713
Info@buybooksontheweb.com
www.buybooksontheweb.com
Toll-free (877) BUY BOOK
Local Phone (610) 941-9999
Fax (610) 941-9959

Printed in the United States of America
Printed on Recycled Paper
Published June 2004

To my friends and family for their patience and encouragement, all my fellow writers in Writer's Den, and most of all to my readers who make it all worth while.

No place, indeed, should murder sanctuarize;
Revenge should have no bounds.

> William Shakespeare (1594-1616)
> *Hamlet* (IV, vii).

Chapter One

Someone once said that everything happens for a reason. Sometimes those reasons aren't exactly clear, but other times, they just walk up and smack you upside the head.

This happened to be the case when I found myself in need of a housekeeper. Since my last case, it seemed everyone needed a private investigator. I felt guilty for not spending as much time with my two dogs, Sydney, my Golden Retriever, and Rambo, my Rottweiler. The house hadn't been cleaned properly in weeks, and the kitchen cabinets held nothing but dog food, coffee, and wine.

You've heard the expression, bachelor pad? Well, I own the feminine version. When I resigned my position as a criminal profiler for the FBI three years ago, after the vicious murder of my partner, Frank Roth, I sought nothing but a quiet, peaceful existence in the small town of Ashley, Michigan. My hometown.

Once a bustling shipping port, Ashley is now a sleepy little lakeside community of close knit, hard working people.

The downtown area of Ashley runs for two blocks and is lined with historically designated storefronts. Washington, the main thoroughfare, ends at a beautiful park located on the shores of Lake St. Clair. Big trees line the sidewalks, and at night, old-fashioned lampposts cast a soft glow on the streets.

I built a three bedroom, two and a half bath split-level. While I thought it too large for just one person, my best friend, Sandra, explained the theory of resale value to me. I didn't understand it all, but here I am, a thirty-something single private detective named Savannah Williams living a quiet life in rural America.

Anyway, in desperate need of a housekeeper, I'd placed an ad in the local paper for a live-in. I keep strange hours, so having someone live in would best suit my needs.

However, as I soon found out, advertising for a housekeeper, and finding a housekeeper are two entirely different things. Most of the women I interviewed took one look at Rambo and headed for the door. The women who stayed were either unqualified, or young women looking for an easy way out of a bad situation with a boyfriend or their family. But as someone else said, when God shuts a door he opens a window.

I'd just finished writing up a report for one of my clients and decided to go eat. I replaced my files in the safe, and after locking up the office, walked down Washington towards the Fisherman's Grill for dinner.

Being late fall, the crisp air took my breath away the moment it hit my lungs. The trees stood bare, and when the breeze blew in from the lake, they would shake, giving them the appearance of shivering in the cold.

A light snow started to fall and the snowflakes glistened like diamonds when they hit the light from the lampposts. I pulled my jacket tighter around my body and hurried down the sidewalk to the warmth of the restaurant.

The Fisherman's Grill is a cozy place with an open floor plan decorated in shades of dark green and burgundy. Various fishing items are displayed throughout, making the restaurant look like an old fishing lodge.

I'd just taken a seat at the bar, when I noticed Jackson Hathaway and an older woman seated at a table.

Jackson is a homicide detective for the Ashley Police Department, and the man I'm currently seeing. My old boyfriend, Jim Matthews, took a job with the FBI in Oregon. The only reason I know that is because he sent me a Dear Jane letter from Portland.

Jackson spotted me, and rose from the table. As he walked towards me, I couldn't help but admire his looks. He stands just less than six feet tall with a stocky, muscular build. His thick hair is dark brown, almost black, and brushed straight back. A perfect backdrop for his olive skin and big, almond shaped brown eyes that compliment his chiseled good looks.

"Hi, I thought you were working late," he said, giving me a quick kiss.

"Hunger got the best of me," I shrugged.

"Come join us," he invited.

"Who's with you?" I asked, looking over at the woman at his table.

"My Mother. She's dying to meet you."

"Oh, great, and I look terrible!" I wailed, looking down at my jeans, black hiking boots, and a black cowl neck sweater.

"You look fine," he sighed, taking my hand and leading me to his table. After pulling out my chair and seating me, he sat down across from his mother.

"Mom, this is Savannah Williams. Savannah, this is my Mother, Lilly Hathaway," Jackson introduced us.

"Hi, Mrs. Hathaway. It's a pleasure to meet you," I smiled.

I judged her to be in her early to middle sixties. Her gray hair, cut short, looked freshly styled. Soft wrinkles creased her forehead and mouth, but it wasn't hard to tell that she'd once been very beautiful. Her piercing blue eyes didn't appear to miss much. While somewhat frail in appearance, I got the distinct impression that she's a force to be reckoned with.

"Savannah. I can call you Savannah can't I? Oh, of course I can, we're practically family. Call me Lilly," she prattled.

"Practically family?" I asked, giving Jackson an inquiring look. "Just what has Jackson told you?"

Before Lilly could answer, the waitress appeared and Jackson ordered me a glass of wine. The waitress handed us menus and we all settled down to decide what to order.

"So, Lilly, are you here for a visit or do you live close by?" I asked.

"I'm moving up here from North Carolina to be closer to Jackson," she explained.

"Oh, how nice. You must be thrilled, Jackson," I said with a sly smile.

"Yes. It'll be nice to have Mom here," he answered through gritted teeth.

"Oh pooh, you just want me up here so you can keep an eye on me. He worries so," Lilly said, directing her last comment towards me.

"I'm sure he does," I said, thinking that she probably gave Jackson good reason to worry.

"So how's the search for a housekeeper going?" Jackson asked, after the server returned with my wine and we placed our orders.

"Not well. There aren't many people who want to live with two big dogs and a neurotic private detective," I sighed.

"You're looking for a live in housekeeper?" Lilly inquired.

"Yes. I'm not home much. I never grocery shop, I can't cook. The dogs are feeling neglected, and my house is a mess!" I exclaimed.

"I'm sure you'll find one," Jackson said soothingly.

"Do your parents live close by dear? Maybe they could take care of the dogs while you're at work," Lilly suggested.

"I wish they did. My parents died in a car accident when I was eleven. I lived with my grandmother until I left for college, and she died a couple of years later," I explained.

"I'm so sorry. You must miss them," Lilly said sympathetically.

"I do," I said quietly, tears welling up in my eyes that I quickly dabbed away with my napkin.

"Oh you poor dear! You have no one," Lilly said.

"She has me," Jackson responded.

"Oh pooh, you work long hours too. You can't take care of this poor child," Lilly snapped.

"Wait. I'm fine. I don't need anyone to take care of me. I need someone to take care of the dogs and the house," I explained.

"Of course," Lilly said, nodding.

"So, you're going to live with Jackson?" I asked.

"No, I'm going to live with you and be your housekeeper, dear," Lilly stated.

"What!" Jackson and I exclaimed.

"But Mom, Savannah hasn't even offered you the job," Jackson exclaimed.

"Of course she hasn't dear. She's much too polite to come right out and ask. But it's obvious she needs me, poor thing," Lilly replied.

5

"I'd love to have you as my housekeeper, but I'm sure Jackson would be terribly disappointed if you didn't live with him," I said in desperation.

"Jackson can take care of himself. You need me. Those dogs need me. No, it's settled. I'll be there in the morning. Jackson will give me directions. So you just stop fretting. Mother Hathaway will take care of everything," Lilly said, patting my hand.

"But don't you have to go back to North Carolina and get your things?" I asked.

"Oh goodness gracious no. I sold practically everything, except for some of the furniture Jackson wanted for his apartment and some small mementos. The movers will be here sometime in the next week or so," Lilly explained.

The waitress returned with our meals, but I'd lost my appetite.

"Lilly, the room for the housekeeper is upstairs. There is a bedroom, a full bathroom, and another bedroom that could be converted to a sitting room. Are the stairs going to be a problem for you?" I asked. Jackson's mother living with me could really complicate things between Jackson and I.

"No, I walk two miles a day. I'm in great shape. I can take the dogs walking with me. It'll do them good to get out and get some exercise," Lilly explained.

"Great. Then I guess it's settled," I said with false gaiety, looking at Jackson for help.

Jackson just shrugged his shoulders and took a bite of his steak in an attempt to conceal the broad grin that spread across his face.

"Yes. Now eat your dinner. Your food's going to get cold," Lilly said.

I quickly ate my dinner, and after giving Lilly the spare key to the house, made a quick exit explaining that the dogs needed to be fed and let outside.

I drove home in a fog, still at a loss as to what just happened.

Chapter Two

I woke up early the next morning still trying to figure out how I'd ended up with Jackson's mother as my new housekeeper. Oh, she seemed sweet enough, but I still wasn't convinced.

I ran around the house straightening things up. I made sure fresh sheets were on the antique cherry bed upstairs and thoroughly dusted and vacuumed the entire second floor. I set out fresh towels and made sure all was in readiness for Lilly's arrival.

I didn't have to wait long. At promptly nine o'clock, Lilly, dressed in a dark blue jogging suit, heavy coat and tennis shoes, arrived with bag and baggage. I opened the door and saw Jackson struggling to get two large suitcases up the porch stairs. Serves him right I thought. He did little to discourage his Mother from moving in.

"Good morning, Dear!" Lilly said brightly as she walked into the house and began to survey her surroundings.

"Good morning. Lilly, Jackson," I said, hiding a laugh as Jackson gave me a dirty look and began trudging his Mother's suitcases up to the second floor.

Sydney and Rambo bounded out of the front room and were in the process of getting acquainted with Lilly.

I found Lilly sitting on the floor petting the dogs and making the appropriate noises over them when I joined her in the kitchen. She'd removed her jacket and hung it over the back of one of the kitchen chairs.

"Would you like a cup of coffee? It's fresh," I offered as I poured another cup for myself.

8

"No thanks, dear. I'll make myself some tea after I get settled," Lilly answered.

"I'll send Jackson to the store then, I don't have any tea, or much else for that matter. I need to go to the grocery store," I apologized.

"No bother. I'll just make a list and go to the store with you. Let me take an inventory of what we need. I can unpack later," she said as she began to open the cupboards and refrigerator.

I watched in amazement as Lilly took a quick inventory, and after digging a pen and small pad of paper out of her enormous purse, began to make out a list for the store.

Jackson rejoined us in the kitchen and poured himself a cup of coffee. Lilly kept bustling around mumbling to herself and writing things down on her notepad.

"Now you two chat for a few minutes while I go upstairs and inspect my quarters. Sydney, Rambo, you come with me you precious little things. Mother Hathaway is here now. You're going to be fine," Lilly cooed. Sydney and Rambo gave Lilly an adoring look before obediently following her upstairs.

"I'm really sorry about this, Savannah," Jackson said choking back a laugh.

"No you're not. You're enjoying every minute of it," I retorted.

Lilly rejoined us in the kitchen and tucked her shopping list into her purse.

"Jackson, you're going to be late for work. Get out of here. Savannah and I have a lot to do today," she said.

"You're right, Mom. You two girls have fun. I'll talk to you both later," he said casting an evil grin towards me. He kissed Lilly good-bye on the cheek and headed for the door.

"Bye, Dear. You be careful. Oh! Jackson! Aren't you forgetting something?" Lilly asked with a frown.

"I don't think so," he said, feeling his pockets for his keys.

"You didn't kiss Savannah good-bye. Goodness, how are you ever going to win this darling child over if you don't kiss her good-bye?" Lilly said.

Jackson walked over and obediently kissed me good-bye before walking out the door.

"I'm sorry, Savannah. I raised him right, I just don't understand what gets into him sometimes," she said, shaking her head sadly.

"Are you ready to go to the store?" I asked.

"Yes, dear. I need to stop by the furniture store too. I want to buy some furniture for the spare bedroom. I know I'm just going to love it here!" she exclaimed, donning her jacket.

Lilly and I got to the furniture store and it didn't take long for her to select a small entertainment center of dark mahogany, a loveseat covered in a sensible navy blue corduroy, and a matching recliner. Lilly also selected a mahogany roll top desk. I offered to buy the furniture for her, but she wouldn't hear of it.

"Jackson's father left me with more money then I could ever spend," she explained handing the salesman her charge card and arranging to have the furniture delivered tomorrow.

On the way to the grocery store, we made a detour to the local appliance store where Lilly purchased a color television and stereo system. After piling her purchases into the backseat of my Jeep, we were on the way to the grocery store.

Two hours later, we arrived home and I carried the groceries into the house and set them on the counter. I lugged the new television and stereo system upstairs and put them in the spare bedroom. Then I called the cable company to arrange to have cable television put in both upstairs bedrooms.

"Do you want me to help you put the groceries away?" I offered.

"Oh no. You go to work. I prefer to set up the kitchen my own way. Have a good day. Dinner's at six. Please be prompt," she answered as she began to reorganize the pantry.

I hastily gathered my things and headed to the office. I got there around noon and began to tackle the mound of paperwork on my desk.

My office is located above what, up until a few months ago, a bakery. However, in my last case I discovered that the owner of the bakery and the building murdered three people and distributed cocaine. He's now serving a life sentence. A young couple, Max and Donna Cummings, bought the building and converted the bakery into a bookstore.

I painted the office a soft mauve and the carpet is a smoky gray Berber with a woven geometric pattern. I found some antique chairs at a flea market and reupholstered them in a mauve and gray floral pattern.

There is an outer office with room for a desk to house a secretary and a few chairs for clients. My office is in the front of the building and contains many windows. A small bathroom is located off the reception area.

There are two ways to access the office. A set of stairs discretely located at the back of the building leads to the outer office. My personal office has a door with stairs leading down the stock room of the bookstore.

I finished up around five and decided to head home and see how Lilly was doing. I drove up to the house and saw Sandra's BMW parked behind Lilly's Intrepid in the driveway.

Sandra is my best friend. She owns her own marketing and advertising business and is quite successful. It's not unusual for her to drop by unannounced and I look forward to her visits.

I walked in the house and saw Lilly and Sandra sitting at the kitchen table. Sandra, wearing a chic black pantsuit, her blonde hair perfectly coiffed, sat hunched over a large book open on the table.

"What do you two have your heads together over?" I asked.

"Oh hi, Savannah. Lilly and I are looking at paint and wallpaper samples for the upstairs," Sandra explained.

"I hope you don't mind," Lilly said.

"No, not at all. It's your space, you can decorate it anyway you want," I assured her.

"That's what your dear friend Sandra said. Now you two chat, I'm going upstairs to see if I like this wallpaper in the bathroom. Oh, by the way, Jackson and Sandra are joining us for dinner," Lilly said as she took the book and headed for the stairs.

"Okay. What smells so good?" I asked taking a big whiff of something delicious cooking in the oven.

"Pot roast. I'll be right back," she answered, disappearing up the stairs.

"Where did you ever find her? She's incredible," Sandra asked, her green eyes sparkling.

I quickly recounted the events of last night and by the time I'd finished Sandra was howling with laughter.

"Good Lord, I thought I'd never see the day someone could handle you like that," she said, wiping the tears of laughter from her eyes.

"Oh, shut up, Sandra," I teased.

"I love her. She's adorable!"

"Who's adorable dear?" Lilly asked as she bustled back into the kitchen.

"You are," Sandra said, as she got up from the table and gave Lilly's shoulders a tight squeeze.

"Oh my no. I'm just a cantankerous old lady," Lilly said, blushing under the praise.

"Can we help with dinner?" I asked.

"No, too many cooks spoil the broth. Besides, you look like hell, dear. You must have worked hard today. Go take a nice shower and change before Jackson gets here. Sandra will help me set the table," Lilly ordered.

Sandra swallowed a laugh as she opened the cabinet to retrieve the plates and glasses. I drew my five-foot tall frame up to its full height before obediently stomping off to my bedroom to take a shower and sulk. I glanced in the mirror while I getting ready for my shower. Lilly was right, I did look like hell. My long, curly auburn hair looked extremely windblown and large bags loomed under my eyes. I needed to get more sleep.

After my shower I dressed and joined Sandra, Jackson, and Lilly in the kitchen. Jackson listened patiently to Lilly recount her many purchases and show him the wallpaper and paint samples.

"Sounds like you two had quite a successful day," he said, handing me a glass of wine and giving me a kiss.

"Yes, we did," I said.

"Dinner's ready," Lilly announced.

We all sat down to the wonderful pot roast and vegetables Lilly prepared. The conversation around the dinner table got quite lively, and I admit I enjoyed myself. Maybe it wouldn't be so bad having Lilly here.

We'd just finished dinner and were helping Lilly clear the table when the doorbell rang.

I padded down the hallway and answered the front door. A middle-aged woman who appeared to have been crying stood on the front stoop. I estimated her to be in her late thirties, early forties, with black shoulder length hair that appeared somewhat disheveled. She looked familiar, but I couldn't place her.

"Are you Savannah Williams?" she asked tentatively.

"Yes. Can I help you?" I answered. Jackson joined me at the front door.

"I'm Amy Conterri. I need to talk to you."

"Please come in," I said, stepping away from the door to allow her to enter.

I led her into my den with Jackson in tow.

"I'm sorry. Do I know you?" I asked once I'd settled her in a chair.

"No, but you know my sister," she explained.

"Your sister?"

"Yes. Madame Phoebe."

"Madame Phoebe. Yes of course. How may I help you?" No wonder she looked familiar, she shared her sister's exotic good looks.

"I found my sister murdered tonight," she blurted out.

"Madame Phoebe! Murdered? How? What happened?" I exclaimed.

"Is everything all right in here?" Lilly asked, as she walked to the door of the den.

"A friend of mine was just found murdered, Lilly," I said.

"Oh my goodness! I'm so sorry. I'll make all of you some tea," Lilly said rushing back toward the kitchen.

"I'm going to make a few phone calls," Jackson said excusing himself.

"Thank you, Jackson. What happened?" I asked, turning my attention back to Amy.

"Who is that man?" she asked.

"Jackson Hathaway. He's a detective for the Ashley Police Department," I replied.

"Oh good. Maybe he can get some answers," she said, dabbing a few tears from her eyes.

"Are you okay, Savannah?" Sandra asked, rushing into the den.

"I'm fine. Now what happened, Amy? Start at the beginning," I prodded.

Sandra settled into a chair listening intently.

"I was supposed to meet Phoebe at the shop at six to go to dinner. I got to the shop and found the door unlocked. I assumed that she'd left it unlocked for me. She closes at five you know."

"Right. Go on," I urged, writing down a few notes on a pad of paper.

"I walked into the shop and found it a mess. It looked like a tornado went through the place. I panicked and started screaming Phoebe's name. She didn't answer. I raced to the back room and saw Phoebe lying on the floor in a pool of blood. She'd been shot. I called the police and while waiting for them, I saw your card on the bulletin board above her desk. I want to know why my sister hired you?" she said.

"Amy, your sister never hired me. We were friends," I answered, handing her a tissue.

"But you're a private detective," she said confused.

"Yes I am. Phoebe helped me out on a few cases and we became friends. Why would anyone want to kill your sister?" I asked.

"I don't know. The police think it was robbery."

Before I could respond Jackson came back into the den.

"Let's get to the shop. I want to take a look around. I just spoke to the Chief of Police in Mt. Clements and got permission to examine the scene. He was more than willing to have us there, once I dropped your name," Jackson said with a small smile.

Lilly re-entered the den carrying a tray with the tea.

"Oh, thanks Lilly, but Jackson and I are heading over to the scene," I said.

"You go ahead. I'll stay here with Ms. Conterri and Sandra. Ms. Conterri shouldn't be alone at a time like this," Lilly said, patting Amy's shoulder.

"Oh, when you get to the store, could you feed Max?" Amy asked.

"Max?" I asked.

"Yes, my sister's cat. I'm going to take him to the Humane Society in the morning. I'm allergic to cats. The poor thing," she explained.

"That's its name?" I asked, remembering the black cat with the beautiful golden eyes.

"Yes, my sister loved that cat."

"Oh my, don't take it to the Humane Society, Dear. The poor creature must be terrified. Savannah, you bring that cat right back to me.

Sandra, go to the store and get whatever we need for a cat. Food, litter box, toys, a bed, well you can figure it out," Lilly ordered.

"I'm on it," Sandra said, hiding a broad grin as she rose from her chair.

"Lilly, I would love to take the cat, but what about the dogs?" I asked.

"The dogs will be fine. They'll have a new playmate," Lilly said confidently.

"Stay here, Amy. I'll be back as soon as I can," I said, realizing in an instant arguing with Lilly would be a losing battle.

"Okay, thanks, Savannah," Amy said.

"You're welcome."

Jackson helped me into my coat and we left to go to Madame Phoebe's New Age Bookstore.

Chapter Three

Jackson and I arrived at the scene in record time. The Chief of the Mt. Clements Police Department had notified the personnel on the scene of our position, and we were immediately granted access.

Upon entering the store I discovered the sweet sickly, smell of death replaced the normal aroma of sandalwood incense.

All the bookshelves lining the walls, usually neatly arranged were now empty; the books lying in tumbled heaps on the floor.

The two dark green and burgundy overstuffed chintz chairs situated in the back corner of the store were sliced open exposing their soft innards of foam and batting.

The glass display cases that once held crystals, incense, tools for Wicca worship, Satan worship, and every other obscure religion, sat smashed open and the contents strewn around the store; the bases of the display cases systematically dismantled.

Evidence technicians busy processing the scene buzzed around the shop like a swarm of bees.

I stopped dead in my tracks at the sight of the devastation, fighting to control my emotions.

Jackson, sensing my struggle, put his arm around my waist.

"Wait here, I'll go find the detective in charge," he whispered in my ear.

"Okay," I said, barely breathing. I watched in silence as Jackson picked his way through the wreckage. He returned a few minutes later.

"Savannah, this is Detective Brent Wilder. Detective, Savannah Williams," Jackson introduced us.

"Ms. Williams, it's a pleasure. I've heard about your work. I just wish we were meeting under different circumstances," he said as we shook hands.

"Thank you, Detective. I do too. What have you got so far?"

"As I understand it, you know that Amy Conterri found her sister in the backroom at about six tonight dead of an apparent gun shot wound. Ms. Conterri claims that she didn't touch anything except for the telephone to call us. Cal Bowers, the Medical Examiner, examined the body and estimates the time of death to be between two and four-thirty this afternoon. He's removed the body to the morgue and will have the results sometime tomorrow. Right now it looks like robbery's the motive for the slaying," Detective Wilder said consulting his notes.

"Thank you, Detective. Can I walk around?" I asked.

"Be my guest."

"Oh, by the way, have you seen a cat?" I asked.

"A cat?"

"Yes, Madam Phoebe had a cat, a big black one. His name is Max. If you find it, could you let me know? He must be scared to death."

"I'll have everyone keep an eye out for it for sure," he answered.

I began to walk through the store, careful not to disturb anything.

Jackson, walking right behind me, cautiously surveyed the damage.

"Jackson, no offense, but could you leave me alone for awhile. I need to work the scene," I asked.

"No problem. I'll help them find the cat," he answered, heading off through the store.

After borrowing a pair of latex gloves from one of the technicians, I spent a good hour walking around the entire store.

After my inspection of the store, I headed to the back room. Entering the back room I saw the chalk line and pool of blood on the floor. I stifled a scream and turned away, leaning on the doorframe to collect myself.

Murder scenes are bad enough to explore, worse if the victim is someone you knew. But I had to do my job. I owed Madame Phoebe that much.

The drawers in Madame Phoebe's desk that held her files stood open, but seemed relatively undisturbed. The table, where Phoebe and I shared many a cup of tea and interesting conversation lay overturned. The pretty yellow tablecloth that once adorned it, now lay on the floor stained with Madame Phoebe's blood and, upon closer examination, two important clues. Footprints.

I'd seen enough. I knew what happened, but I didn't know why.

I walked out of the office and rejoined Jackson and Detective Wilder.

"Well?" Jackson said.

"This was not a robbery."

"Are you sure?" Detective Wilder asked.

I'm sure," I said walking over to the front windows of the store and peeking out the blinds.

"I'll explain in a minute, but first I think you should get some men to secure the area outside the building. The press has arrived and are circling like vultures."

"Shit," Detective Wilder said, looking out the front door.

Detective Wilder disappeared outside and I heard him barking orders to the uniformed officers on the scene.

"Okay, you were saying?" Detective Wilder said, rejoining Jackson and I.

"Whoever killed Madame Phoebe was looking for something specific. I don't think they found it. They probably threatened Madame Phoebe, but she wouldn't tell them anything. Judging from the back room, she must have put up quite a struggle before they shot her," I answered.

"Interesting. Go on," he urged.

"My guess is that they killed Madame Phoebe and then tore the store apart looking for whatever they'd come to get. If robbery was the motive, there would have been no reason to cut open the cushions on the chairs, or practically dismantle the display cases."

"Good point. So what makes you think they didn't find what they were looking for?" Detective Wilder asked.

"Because of the pattern of destruction. Take a look around. The destruction varies in degree. For example, the books, they weren't even searched. That tells us that they weren't looking for a piece of paper or money. They were looking for something bigger. The books were thrown off the shelves out of frustration, or to make it look like a robbery, frustration would be my guess though. Thieves do not dismantle display cases; they simply smash the glass and grab anything of value. No, whoever did this was definitely looking for something, and they were very methodical. They started with the display cases and worked their way around the store, their frustration growing by leaps and bounds," I explained.

"Okay. Anything else?" Detective Wilder asked, furiously scribbling down notes in a little black notebook.

"Yes. My guess is that the time of death is closer to four. It would take forty-five minutes to an hour to do this type of damage."

"You keep saying they, are you sure there was more than one person?" Detective Wilder asked.

"Positive. I know your Crime Scene Unit hasn't had time to process the back room yet, but there are two footprints in blood on the tablecloth on the floor. I know that Cal or your crew would never be so careless, as to step in blood and track it all over the place. Yet, I didn't see any footprints in the pool of blood. Interesting. Although I did notice that the floor is uneven. It's not impossible for the blood to have pooled over the footprints. The shoes are different sizes and I know neither print belongs to Amy Conterri. She's wearing high-heeled black boots. These prints resemble a man's dress shoe and some type of flat boot and are too large to belong to a woman," I answered.

"Good. Okay. I'll alert the team to start processing the back room. Thanks for your help," Detective Wilder said.

"My pleasure," I answered.

"Ms. Williams?" One of the Crime Scene technicians said approaching me.

"Yes?"

"We found the cat, but we can't get near him. He's scared and hisses at us every time we try to pick him up.

"Great. Where is he?"

"I'll show you," he answered.

Following him to the back of the store I saw the petrified black cat on top of one of the bookshelves. The technician, who'd retrieved a small stepladder, had been trying in vain to get him down.

I climbed up the ladder and looked at Max. His eyes were open wide and filled with fear. His ears were lying flat, and he'd puffed his fur out to make him look twice his normal size.

"Max, sweetie, come on, honey. I'm going to take you home," I cooed, reaching out to pick him up.

He must have recognized me, because he willingly let me pick him up and clung to me tightly. I winced as his claws pierced through my sweater into my skin. Jackson steadied me as I climbed down the ladder. I spent a few minutes talking to him softly and caressing his head. He soon stopped shaking, cuddled up against me, and thankfully withdrew his claws from my chest.

"Let's get him out of here," Jackson said putting his arm around me.

"Okay. Hang on a second though."

I walked over to Detective Wilder.

"I'm going to want access to the scene when your personnel is finished. Is that going to be a problem?" I asked.

"Not at all. Just call the station and I'll come over and let you in anytime you want. Do you have a card so I can contact you?" he asked.

"Yes. Jackson, could you please get a card out of the front section of my bag. Jackson retrieved the card and handed it to Detective Wilder.

"Oh, and by the way, if you see Ms. Conterri tell her I'm going to want to talk to her," Detective Wilder said.

"I'm sure she'll cooperate any way she can. But could you wait and talk to her in the morning. She's quite shaken," I responded.

"No problem. Thanks again," Detective Wilder said, opening the front door for Jackson and I.

As we exited, reporters immediately surrounded us. I felt the cat stiffen in fear and dig his claws into my skin. The reporters were hitting us both with a barrage of questions.

Two police officers quickly came to our rescue and escorted us to Jackson's truck.

By the time we got back to my place I was exhausted. The cat had fallen asleep on my lap, and I gently carried him into the house.

"Oh, goodness. Look at that beautiful creature," Lilly said, taking the cat from me.

"He's probably hungry," I said.

"Come on, Sweetie, Mother Hathaway has got some nice food for you, then you can meet your new playmates," Lilly said disappearing into the kitchen.

I headed into the den. I had a lot more questions for Amy Conterri.

"What did you find out?" Amy asked me anxiously as I joined her and Sandra.

"Amy, when did you last talk to Phoebe," I asked, ignoring her question.

"Yesterday afternoon. Why?"

"What did you two talk about?"

"Let me think for a second," Amy said, scrunching her face up in thought.

"Can I get anybody anything?" Lilly asked, sticking her head into the den.

"Yes. Could you get me a glass of wine please? Amy? Sandra? You want anything?" I asked.

"Wine's fine for me," Sandra answered.

"Nothing for me, thank you," Amy said.

"How's the cat?" I asked before Lilly left to retrieve the wine.

"Eating like a horse. Poor thing," Lilly answered, scooting off to the kitchen.

"To answer your question. Phoebe and I just talked about the usual stuff, you know, how business was in the store, making plans for the holidays, and then we made our plans to have dinner tonight," Amy answered.

"Did she mention anything else?" I prodded.

"Like what?" Amy asked.

"Anything. Did she say she had errands to run, or about getting something new for the shop? Did she seem scared or worried about anything?"

"No, she seemed fine to me. She did mention that she had to run to the post office this morning before she opened the store, but that's not unusual. Phoebe had many out of state customers and she regularly mailed them their orders," Amy replied.

Lilly returned to the den with the wine and I gratefully took a long sip.

"I'm going to let the dogs in now and introduce them to Max. I'll just shut the door to the den so you won't be disturbed," Lilly said.

Sandra, Amy, Jackson and I immediately leapt out of our chairs and watched out the glass doors of the den as Rambo and Sydney were introduced to the cat.

Much to my surprise, neither the cat or the dogs seemed very impressed with each other, and after a couple of minutes of hissing and barking, they all settled down peacefully. I breathed a sigh of relief.

"The police are going to want to talk to you again Amy, but not until tomorrow," I informed her.

"Okay. But I already told them everything."

"I'm sure you did, but talk to them anyway," I said firmly.

"Okay, I will," she said.

I showed her to the door.

"Take care of yourself, Amy."

"I will. I still can't believe it. Not that Phoebe and I were real close, but she was my sister. I'm going to miss her," she said, her eyes welling up with tears.

"Are you going to be okay to drive, or would you like me to get Sandra or Jackson to drive you home?"

"I'll be fine," she answered, giving my hand a quick squeeze. "Night."

"Night," I answered, and watched Amy walk slowly down the front walk to her car.

"Okay, Sandra. Give me the lowdown. How did Amy act after I left?" I asked, walking back into the den followed by Lilly. I lit up a cigarette and flopped into my chair.

"She really seemed upset Savannah. Why?"

"I don't think she's being completely honest with me."

"I agree with Savannah. I think she's hiding something," Lilly said.

"Really? What makes you think that?" I asked.

"Nothing I can put my finger on, just an impression you know. I could be wrong," Lilly answered.

"I don't think you're wrong, Lilly. I got that impression too," I agreed.

We sat in the den reminiscing about Madame Phoebe and engaging in that annoying small talk that occurs when no one really has much to say, but can't stand the silence.

"Look at the time! I'm going to bed. Savannah, dear, don't stay up too late you need your rest," Lilly chided rising from her chair.

"Oh wow. It is late. I'm sorry, Savannah. Talk to you later. Night Mom. Night Sandra," Jackson said, and after giving me a kiss, headed back to his apartment.

"So what's your next move?" Sandra asked as I walked her to the door.

"I'm convinced that whoever killed Madame Phoebe was after something specific. I'm going to find out what it is," I answered.

Little did I know that I wouldn't have to look very hard.

Chapter Four

I woke up the next morning covered in animals. Sydney and Rambo were both sleeping on the bed, and Max lay curled up on my pillow. When I opened my eyes I found myself being stared at by his gorgeous gold eyes.

"Morning, Sweetie," I said, giving him a scratch behind the ears.

Max stretched luxuriously and began to purr. I snuggled with him for a few more minutes before being coaxed out of bed by the smell of fresh coffee and bacon.

I put on my black chenille robe and walked down the hallway towards the kitchen.

Lilly looked adorable standing at the stove in her yellow terry cloth robe and fuzzy brown bunny slippers.

"Morning, Lilly," I said, reaching for a coffee cup.

"Oh! Morning, Savannah. How are you feeling, dear?" she asked popping two slices of bread into the toaster.

"I'm okay. How'd you sleep?"

"Like a baby. That bed is so comfortable. How do you want your eggs?" she asked, pulling a couple of plates from the cabinet.

"No eggs for me, just bacon and toast," I answered sitting down at the table.

Sydney and Rambo had followed me out of the bedroom and I let them out the sliding glass door into the back yard.

"Have you seen Max this morning? I couldn't find him anywhere," Lilly fretted.

"Last time I saw him he was curled up on my pillow sleeping," I answered with a chuckle.

"Well, I'll let the poor thing sleep, I'm sure when he's hungry he'll come looking for me," she said, buttering a piece of toast.

"I'm sure he will. Judging by the size of that cat I don't think he's missed many meals," I laughed.

Lilly chuckled as she put our plates on the table and we settled down to have breakfast.

"Would you mind if I turned on the television? I like to keep current."

"Go ahead. I'm interested to see if there's any news on Madame Phoebe's murder," I replied.

Lilly grabbed the remote control from on top of the television on the kitchen counter, and turned on the news.

We were just in time to hear the following broadcast:

> "Phoebe Conterri, better known as Madam Phoebe, was found brutally murdered in her store yesterday afternoon. We have a clip from the news conference held by Detective Brent Wilder of the Mt. Clements Police Department last night."

I saw Detective Wilder appear on the screen standing in front of Madame Phoebe's store.

"What was the motive for the slaying?" A reporter asked.

"This investigation is just starting. I have no comment on that at this time," Detective Wilder answered evasively.

"Is the rumor true that criminal profiler and private detective, Savannah Williams, has been hired to assist in the investigation?" Another reporter asked.

"No, not in a official capacity," Detective Wilder said.

The clip ended and returned to the newscaster.

"The community is shocked and saddened at the news of Ms. Conterri's death. Funeral arrangements are pending and we will continue to follow this developing story." The newscaster concluded.

"Damn," I whispered as the segment ended.

"What's wrong, Dear?" Lilly asked sipping her tea.

"If the press even suspects that I am involved in an investigation they will be hounding me for information."

"Well, I pity the reporter that shows up here!" she said fiercely. "Don't you worry, I'll take care of them with no problem."

"I'm sure you will," I said stifling a laugh. I could picture Lilly marching indignantly out on the front porch and shooing away the reporters. Hope I was here to see that.

"Now you go get ready for work. I'll take care of the breakfast dishes," she said, rising from the table and clearing away the plates.

"Okay. Thanks."

Before I left for the office, I wrote down my office number on a pad of paper for Lilly told her to call me if she needed anything.

I made it into town about nine and took the back stairs up to my office, avoiding the hordes of reporters gathered in front of the building. It was going to be a long day.

I started a pot of coffee and sat down to open a file on Phoebe's murder. I spent a considerable amount of time typing up what I'd learned from the crime scene. I'd just finished, when the telephone rang.

"Savannah Williams," I answered cautiously.

"Hi, Savannah," Jackson said.

"Hi, Jackson. Thank God it's you. I thought it might be a reporter."

"Yeah, you sure know how to draw a crowd," he teased.

"Oh, hush, or I'll sic your Mother on you!" I threatened.

"Okay, okay, I give. I just got off the phone with my Mom as a matter of fact. She's worried about you. She said that you weren't real happy about the news reports this morning. I told her I'd keep an eye on you today and that made her feel better. Do you want me to have a couple officers go chase away the reporters?"

"No, they're just doing their job, besides, I'm going to call Detective Wilder and have another look at the crime scene now that the evidence techs are out of the way."

"Okay. Let me know if you need anything."

"Okay. Thanks. Talk to you later," I answered.

After hanging up the phone I began to tackle the stack of mail sitting on my desk. When the telephone rang I just about jumped out of my skin.

"Savannah Williams," I answered.

"Hi, its Amy Conterri."

"Hi, Amy, what's up?" I asked.

"Detective Wilder stopped by my apartment this morning," she stated.

"Oh?"

31

"He asked me a whole bunch of questions. Like where I was when Phoebe was murdered and if anyone can verify my whereabouts."

"What did you tell him?"

"I was home alone. I can't prove it, but I was!" she wailed.

"It's okay. Just calm down. Amy, whoever killed Phoebe was looking for something very specific. I need you to think back and try to remember if Phoebe said anything that could give me a clue as to what they were looking for."

"I can't think of a thing," she said after a small pause.

"Just call me if you remember something."

"Okay. Thanks. Anyway, I better get going. I have a lot to take care of. Oh, the police were nice enough to send someone in to clean up the backroom of Phoebe's store. Are you planning on going back there today?"

"Yes. As a matter of fact I am. Thanks for the info."

"Keep in touch," she said.

"I will. Bye Amy."

I hung up the phone, lit up a cigarette and sat back to think. There's something she wasn't telling me. I spent a few minutes deep in thought about what secret Amy could be hiding, when the telephone rang and snapped me back into reality.

"Savannah Williams," I said, absently as I answered the phone.

"Savannah, Dear, a package was just delivered for you," Lilly breathed excitedly.

"Thank you, Lilly. I'll open it when I get home," I replied, rather irritated.

"No, Dear, you don't understand. The package is from Madame Phoebe and it was mailed yesterday!" she exclaimed.

"I'm on the way," I said, and without waiting for a reply, hung up the phone.

I quickly closed up my office and bolted down the stairs to my Jeep. I cut through back streets to avoid the press and made it home in record time.

Lilly stood waiting for me as I came through the garage door into the laundry room.

"I put the package on your desk," Lilly said, following me into my den.

I walked into my den and saw a box sitting on my desk. It stood about a foot and a half tall and approximately a foot wide.

Lilly watched in anticipation as I opened it. When I got the box open, I was met with a piece of solid foam about three or four inches thick. Underneath the foam sat an envelope that said "Savannah".

I set aside the envelope and pulled out a skull that appeared to be made out of some type of cloudy crystal and close in size to a human skull. The teeth were perfectly carved and the entire skull appeared to be anatomically correct.

I heard Lilly inhale sharply as she caught sight of the skull.

"What is it?" she asked, her voice barely above a whisper.

"A skull?" I replied puzzled.

"I know that! But what does it mean?"

"I have no clue. Maybe the letter will shed some light on our friend," I said wryly, reaching for the envelope.

I opened the envelope and pulled out a piece of neatly folded stationary and began to read the letter. It said:

Savannah,

You are the only person I can trust to keep this skull safe. Stop by the shop after you receive this and I will explain.

                              Madame Phoebe

"Well, that doesn't help much," Lilly said in disgust.

"Actually, Lilly, it helps more than you know," I said.

Before Lilly could reply, the doorbell rang. It was the furniture store. Lilly bustled about giving the deliverymen directions on where to place her new furniture.

I took the opportunity of her being distracted to re-read Madame Phoebe's letter. I placed the letter and the skull back in the box and placed it in the large antique bank safe that is housed on the second floor of my den.

My den is two stories tall. The first floor consists of a very large, antique library table that I use as a desk, as well as several file cabinets that are stuffed with files of old cases and other information from when I worked at the FBI. My computer sits on a small, antique mahogany table alongside my desk. Luxurious hunter green and gold oriental rugs grace the hardwood floors. The second story of the den is lined with bookshelves. A spiral staircase was installed that winds up to a catwalk so that I have access to the bookshelves and the safe.

I called the Mt. Clements Police Department and had a short discussion with Detective Wilder.

"Lilly! I'll be back later!" I yelled up the stairs. The furniture deliverymen had left, and Lilly was upstairs setting up her sitting room.

"Dinner's at six. Call if you're going to be late."

"Okay. See you later."

I met Detective Wilder at Madame Phoebe's shop and he graciously unlocked the door and allowed me to enter ahead of him. It took both of us a few minutes to find the light switches, but soon the store became bathed in light.

"Listen, I talked to the Chief this morning. He wondered if you'd be interested in consulting on this case; at your usual rate of course," he said.

"That'd be great considering I have no intention of letting this thing go until I find out who killed Phoebe," I answered.

"I figured as much," he laughed. "Oh, I stopped on the way and made you a spare key to the shop."

"Thanks." I said, adding the key to my key ring.

"I have to go, but I'll catch up with you later," he said, walking towards the door.

"Okay. Lock the door on your way out please."

"Sure thing."

I heard the decisive click of a deadbolt sliding into place behind him as he left.

To search the store again would be useless. Any information about the skull would more than likely be in the file cabinet located in the backroom.

The blood no longer lay on the floor and I noticed that the evidence technicians removed the yellow tablecloth.

I performed a thorough search of Madame Phoebe's desk, but came up empty. I then placed a call to Detective Wilder to gain permission to remove the files from the store. It would be easier to go through them at home.

I found a few shipping boxes, similar to the one Madame Phoebe used for the statue, and soon had all the files in the boxes and loaded in my Jeep. After securing the store, I headed home.

Chapter Five

I arrived home to find Lilly and the dogs gone and Max lying peacefully on the couch. He gave me a lazy stare and stretched before settling back down to his nap. Obviously he'd settled into his new home without difficulty.

I schlepped in the two boxes of files from Madame Phoebe's and deposited them on my desk in my den. After starting a pot of coffee, I went upstairs to look at Lilly's sitting room.

The new loveseat sat against the far wall. The entertainment system sat across from the loveseat, and Lilly already hooked up her television and stereo. The cable company must have been here, because a cable box rested on top of the television. Lilly put the roll top desk in front of the window and already filled a few of the nooks and crannies.

I heard the familiar gurgle of the coffee pot signaling that my coffee was ready, so I skipped down the stairs. As I poured my coffee, I noticed a plate of chocolate chip cookies on the counter. I grabbed a couple and headed into my den. Okay, I thought as I bit into one of the cookies, having Lilly here definitely could have its advantages. Happily dipping my cookie into my coffee, I settled down to go through Madame Phoebe's files.

After about a half hour two things became crystal clear. Madame Phoebe had no discernable filing system, and I had no clue what I was looking for.

Before I knew it, two hours passed and I still hadn't found anything useful and Lilly and the dogs still weren't home.

I picked up the phone and dialed Jackson's number.

"Ashley Detective Bureau, Detective Hathaway," Jackson said into the phone.

"Hi, its Savannah. Have you heard from your Mom today?"

"Yeah, she called this morning and invited me for dinner. Why?"

"Her and dogs are gone. I got home almost three hours ago. I'm getting kind of worried."

"I'm sure she's fine. She probably just took the dogs with her on some errands."

"You think?" I said skeptically.

"Listen, if she's not back in another couple hours call me."

"Okay. See you later," I answered, feeling better.

"See you at dinner. Bye," he said and hung up the phone.

I went into the kitchen for another cup of coffee when I heard the garage door opening. I'd given Lilly the extra garage door opener for her car. A couple of minutes later the dogs bounded into the house followed by Lilly.

"Lilly, oh thank God. I was worried half to death. Where have you been?"

"The dogs and I just ran a few errands, Dear. How was your day?" she asked, moving around the kitchen preparing dinner.

"Fine. Do you need any help?"

"No. Go back to what you were doing," she said dismissively.

"Lilly. I have to ask you a favor," I said pensively.

"What is it, Dear?" she said, giving me her full attention.

"The work I do is very confidential and private. Please don't say anything to anybody about what I am working on. Okay?" I said.

"Oh, of course not. Jackson's father taught me that you know."

"Jackson's father?"

"Yes. Didn't Jackson tell you?" she asked in amazement.

"Tell me what?"

"That his father was an FBI agent of course."

"He was? Jackson never mentioned his father before."

"Quite understandable. Jackson and his father didn't get on very well. But that's a story for another time. I have to get dinner ready."

"Okay. I'll be in my den if you need me," I answered, deep in thought.

Without waiting for Lilly to answer, I returned to my den and began going back through Madame Phoebe's papers.

By five-thirty I'd all but given up hope of finding anything useful. Then I came across a letter that could give me the break I'd been looking for. The stationary was from the Museum of Ancient History located in Mt. Clements and dated almost two weeks ago. The letter, handwritten, read:

My Dearest Phoebe,

Thank you for agreeing to ensure the safety of the skull. Just knowing that it will not fall into the hands of DePaulo gives me great relief. As per our agreement, I will have no knowledge of whom you are going to entrust with its safety. Please take extra precautions to make sure you're safe. DePaulo will stop at nothing to gain possession of the skull. I hate that I have to put you in this kind of danger my dear Phoebe, but I have no other recourse. I fear that DePaulo may have already learned that I'm in possession of the skull. As you are well aware, news travels fast in the world of antiquities and I don't dare display it until I know DePaulo is out of the picture.

Stay safe, Phoebe.

Yours always,
Arthur

I reread the letter twice to make sure I'd gleaned every bit of information. Questions began racing through my head so fast, I couldn't slow them down long enough to even begin to formulate answers.

However, something in the letter sparked off a vague note of recognition. I remembered reading something about the Museum of Ancient History in the newspaper last week.

"Lilly?" I yelled into the kitchen.

"Yes, Dear?" she said, walking in the den wiping her hands on a dishtowel.

"Could you run out to the garage and bring me last weeks Macomb Tribune from the recycling bin please?"

"Of course," she said, and hurried off to retrieve the newspapers.

While waiting for Lilly to return, I carefully folded the letter and placed it in the safe with the skull.

I'd just gotten back to my chair when Lilly returned with the newspapers and sat them on my desk.

"Jackson should be here any second. Dinner is in fifteen minutes," she said, quietly slipping from the room.

"Okay. Thanks, Lilly," I answered as I began to thumb through the newspaper.

It only took a minute or two to find the story I was looking for. According to the paper, there'd been a break-in at Museum of Ancient History last Friday. Although thoroughly searched, nothing was stolen. Police suspected an inside job because the intruder bypassed the security system.

The article went on to say that the Museum of Ancient History has had its share of tragedies the past two weeks.

Its curator, Arthur Friedman, died in a car accident only a week before, and now the apparent break-in.

"How interesting," I said, setting aside the newspaper.

"What's interesting?" Jackson asked, walking into the den and giving me a lingering kiss.

I'd been so lost in the newspaper article I hadn't even heard the doorbell ring.

"You're a lot more interesting than what I was doing," I said rising from my chair and into his arms.

Lilly interrupted a long, luxurious kiss by announcing that dinner was ready. Reluctantly, Jackson and I broke apart and headed into the dining area to eat.

Lilly had prepared broiled salmon, steamed asparagus, and a fresh, crisp salad. For dessert we enjoyed the perfectly diced fresh fruit with whipped cream.

"Lilly, dinner was incredible," I said, as I sat back from the table.

"Thank you," She said, blushing at the praise. "Now you two go into the den. I know you have a lot to talk about. I'll bring some coffee in to you as soon as I've cleaned the kitchen."

Jackson and I obediently marched into the den shutting the French doors behind us. I was anxious to talk to him about what I'd found.

I spent the next fifteen minutes showing Jackson the skull, the letter Phoebe received from Arthur Friedman, and the newspaper article. Jackson listened carefully and without interruption until I'd finished.

"I agree that whoever killed Madame Phoebe and broke into the museum was looking for this skull. But who's DePaulo?" he asked.

"I don't know."

"Have you told Detective Wilder about any of this?"

"Not yet, but I plan on talking to him tomorrow. The Mt. Clements Police Department hired me as a consultant. I'm a little worried though."

"Worried? How?" Jackson asked.

"Well, you know as well as I do that every police department has leaks. If DePaulo or whoever did all this gets wind that we are onto them, or finds out I have the skull, they might come after me. I just can't risk it. Not with your Mom living here."

"You're right. It's too dangerous. Damn it, Savannah, how do you get yourself into these messes?" he asked, running his hands through his hair in frustration.

"I wish I knew," I said, laughing.

"In the meantime, watch your back and fly low for awhile," he said seriously.

"I will," I said as I put everything back into the safe.

"What's your next move?"

"I'm going to go see the assistant curator at the museum tomorrow. I'm hoping he can answer a lot of questions."

"Let me know what you find out."

Before I could answer, Lilly came into the den with coffee.

"I'm going upstairs you two. Have a good night," she said with a sly smile.

"Okay. Night," Jackson and I responded.

Jackson and I watched Lilly go up the stairs to her sitting room and shut the door.

"Subtlety is not her specialty," he said laughing.

"I noticed that," I chuckled.

Jackson and I closed up the den and while I let the dogs out, Jackson poured us a glass of wine. We settled onto the couch to watch a movie. I think I saw the first half hour before falling asleep.

When I woke up, Jackson was carrying me into the bedroom.

"What time is it?" I asked, wiping the sleep out of my eyes.

"Eleven. Let's go to bed," Jackson said, softly kissing my neck.

"With your Mother in the house?"

"We'll just have to be quiet," he whispered as he helped me get undressed and into bed.

An hour later, I drifted off to sleep in Jackson's arms.

Chapter Six

I woke up to a gentle tapping at the bedroom door.

"Savannah, Jackson, breakfast in fifteen minutes," Lilly said through the closed door.

"Okay, Lilly. Thanks." I said, nudging Jackson awake.

"Huh? What?" he mumbled, barely opening his eyes.

"Breakfast."

"Oh, okay. Do you want to shower first?" he asked, rubbing his eyes.

"No, you have to leave before I do. Go ahead," I answered, snuggling farther under the covers.

Jackson crawled out of bed with a sigh and headed for the bathroom. I waited until I heard the water running in the shower before getting out of bed. I donned my black robe laying over the end of the bed and headed out in the kitchen to get a cup of coffee.

"Morning. Did you sleep well?" Lilly said sweetly, hiding a smile.

"Just fine," I said, not taking the bait. I poured myself a cup of coffee and walked back into my bedroom. Sydney and Rambo followed and leapt onto the bed.

I spent a few minutes petting them while waiting for Jackson to get out of the shower.

Finally, Jackson emerged from the bathroom with a towel around his waist and took my coffee out of my hand.

After taking a long sip, he handed me back the empty cup and started to get dressed.

"Hey! You drank all my coffee!" I protested.

"Sorry, but I worked up a powerful thirst last night," he said with a wink.

I threw a pillow at him and stalked into the bathroom.

It took me longer than usual to decide what to wear. Normally I would just throw on a pair of jeans and a sweatshirt, but I wanted to look nice when I went to the museum this morning. I finally decided on a pair of khaki pants, navy blue angora sweater, navy blue knee socks and a pair of penny loafers. Then joined Jackson and Lilly in the kitchen.

"Oh, you look nice, Savannah! Doesn't she look nice Jackson?" Lilly prodded as she poured me another cup of coffee.

"She looks incredible as always," he said smiling.

"Thank you, Jackson," I said, blushing slightly.

I sat down at the table and Lilly served up a big breakfast of ham and cheese omelets and toast.

Max sauntered into the kitchen and jumped up on the counter to get his breakfast.

"Lilly, why is the cat food on the counter?" I asked.

"Because the dogs will eat it if I put it on the floor," Lilly explained. "Besides dear, cats are such clean creatures. I was sure you wouldn't mind."

"Like she had a choice." Jackson murmured quietly.

"Oh now hush, Jackson!" Lilly said, slapping him on the arm.

"No. It's okay," I said, trying to smooth things over.

Jackson ate breakfast quickly and after kissing Lilly and I good bye, left for work.

As I let Jackson out the front door, I saw Sandra's BMW pull in the driveway.

"Hi! What are you doing here so early?" I asked as I led Sandra into the kitchen.

"Lilly and I are going shopping today. Didn't she tell you? She told me to come for breakfast," Sandra said as she sat down at the table.

Lilly poured Sandra a cup of coffee and started to make her an omelet.

"Oh really? What are you two shopping for today?" I asked.

"Accessories!" Sandra said, her emerald eyes shining.

"For what?"

"Her bedroom and sitting room," she explained, munching on a piece of toast.

"Oh, that should be fun."

"Want to come with?" Sandra asked.

"I wish I could, but I have a busy day."

"Oh? Anything interesting?"

"I have to go to the Museum of Ancient History in Mt. Clements."

"Oh. What for? You know I do their advertising and marketing don't you?"

"You do? I didn't know that. What can you tell me about the museum?" I asked with great interest.

"Well, the curator, Arthur Friedman, was killed in a car accident a little over a week ago. His son, Paul, the assistant curator, has taken over his father's position. Paul called me earlier this week as a matter of fact to tell me about the break-in."

"Tell me about Paul."

"Oh, he's very handsome and very nice, just like his father," she said.

"Okay, now give me details," I teased.

"Well, there's not much to tell really. He's very competent to run the museum, that's for sure. In fact, Paul and I have been dating for the last month."

"You have! Why didn't you say anything?" I stammered.

"Savannah, if you remember, you were very busy on a case and we barely saw each other."

"You're right. I'm sorry. I need to get in to see Paul Friedman today. Think you can help?"

"Oh, of course. I'll call him after breakfast and set it up. Does this have to do with Madame Phoebe's death?" she asked.

"Sandra, I'm not sure. Even if I was, you know I couldn't tell you."

"I know, client confidentiality and all that. Damn that gets in the way of good gossip," she said.

"I know. But don't you go pumping Paul for information either. I mean it, Sandra! Whoever is behind Madame Phoebe's death isn't playing games. Understand?" I said firmly.

"That doesn't sound good, Savannah. This is going to get dangerous isn't it?" she said with a worried look on her face.

"It has the potential to. That's why it's so important that you stay out of this."

"I don't like the sound of that, Savannah," Lilly said as she set Sandra's omelet on the table.

"I'm sorry, Lilly. That goes for you too. The less you two know, the safer you will be."

"I understand, Dear," Lilly said.

"Me too," Sandra added begrudgingly.

"Okay. Good."

I joined Sandra for another cup of coffee while she devoured her breakfast. After breakfast, Sandra called Paul Friedman and arranged to have him meet me at the museum in an hour.

I left Sandra and Lilly huddled over the kitchen table looking at sales flyers and headed over to the museum. I had no clue what I was going to say, or how much I was going to tell Paul Friedman. My goal was to basically get him talking and just sit back and listen.

I arrived at the Museum of Ancient History, and parked in front of the building.

The museum mimicked Greek architecture and is constructed out of white marble that had darkened with age. A set of marble steps led up to the front entrance and large pillars graced the expansive front entranceway.

I walked into the museum and gave my name to the woman sitting at the Information Desk.

A couple of minutes later I saw a man I assumed to be Paul Friedman walking toward me.

Sandra was right. He is handsome. I judged him to be about five foot ten and his sandy blond hair was cut very conservatively. Dressed in black dress pants, gray shirt, and a double-breasted matching suit coat he carved out an impressive figure.

As he got closer, I noticed that he had deep blue eyes and lush, thick eyelashes.

Paul spotted me and flashed me a smile of very white, very perfect teeth. He's definitely Sandra's type.

"Ms. Williams?" Paul asked, extending his hand.

"Yes. Mr. Friedman?" I asked, shaking his hand.

"Please call me Paul," he said, in a pleasant voice.

"Thank you. Call me Savannah."

"This way please," he said, graciously taking my elbow to lead me to his office.

Paul's office sat just off the main lobby of the museum. It's expansive, with a large cherry wood desk, and several library tables that held various antiquities. Strategically placed luxurious oriental rugs accented the highly polished wood floors.

Paul led me to an overstuffed black leather wing backed chair and after I was seated, walked around his desk and sat down.

"Would you like some coffee or perhaps tea?" he asked gallantly.

"Coffee, please."

Paul picked up his telephone and asked that coffee for two be brought to his office. Then he turned his attention to me.

"Sandra spoke very highly of you. She said that you're former FBI and that you're working as a private detective now," he said.

"Thank you. Yes. That's true."

A soft knock sounded at the door and a young woman entered the office carrying a sterling silver tray with matching coffee pot, two coffee mugs and a cream and sugar set.

She sat the coffee down on Paul's desk and discreetly exited the office, quietly closing the door behind her.

He poured the coffee and extended a steaming mug to me.

"Thank you," I said, taking the mug from his hands.

"Now, what can I do for you, Savannah?" he asked, taking a sip of his coffee.

49

"First, I'm sorry to hear about your father."

"Thank you. It was a tragic accident," Paul said with a hint of sarcasm to his voice.

"You don't think it was an accident?"

"Why would you say that?" he asked, his eyes narrowing.

"Oh, no reason. Just the tone of your voice."

"I'm sorry, Savannah. It's just with the death of my father, and the recent break-in at the museum, I'm under a lot of stress."

"Yes, I'm sure you are. Tell me about the break-in," I prodded.

"It was last Friday. I was the last one out of the museum, as usual. I know I locked the doors and set the alarm. The night watchman called in sick, so I made sure everything was secure. When the day watchman got to the museum on Friday morning, he discovered the break-in."

"And nothing was taken?"

"No. That's the strange thing. My father's and my offices were in shambles as well as the storage room and basement. But the museum displays were untouched."

"So, what were they looking for then?" I asked leaning forward.

"What makes you think they were looking for something specific?" he asked suspiciously.

"It's obvious. They were looking for the skull, weren't they Paul?" I asked, deciding to drop a bombshell. I was sick of the dance, and just wanted to get down to the facts.

"How, how do you know about the skull?" he asked, fear filling his eyes.

"Because a good friend of your father's and mine was murdered for it."

"Who?" he asked, trying to regain his composure.

"Phoebe Conterri."

"Madame Phoebe? Murdered?"

"Yes, a couple of days ago. Don't you watch the news?"

"I saw the story. I just didn't put it together until now. I know my father and her were quite close, but I never met her. What do you mean she was murdered for the skull?" he asked.

I pulled the letter from Arthur Friedman to Madame Phoebe out of my bag and handed it to Paul.

I watched his expression turn from curiosity to shock as he read the letter. When he finished reading it he handed it back across his desk to me. I noticed his hands were shaking.

"Did DePaulo get the skull?" he asked.

"I don't think so. Now, why don't we quit doing this tap dance and exchange information, Paul? Want me to start? Okay. First of all, I don't think your father's death was an accident. Secondly, whoever broke into the museum was looking for the skull. Thirdly, those same people probably killed Madame Phoebe for it. Now, why don't you tell me what really happened to your father, who DePaulo is, and why that skull is worth killing for?"

Paul took a sip of coffee and composed himself before speaking.

To answer your questions, DePaulo is an arts and antiquities dealer. I know of him only by reputation, which is not favorable. But that's not unusual. My father ran the business end of the museum until his death. My primary responsibility is the day to day operations and the setting up of new exhibits."

"Tell me about your father's accident."

"He was on his way home. It was snowing quite heavily. The police said his car slid off the road and down an embankment into the path of a semi. He died instantly."

"There was no investigation?"

"The police didn't see the need. You think he was murdered don't you?" he said, his blue eyes staring at me intently.

"Yes. I do," I said, meeting his gaze. "Tell me about his state of mind recently. Did he seem scared? Worried?"

"Come to think of it. He did seem a little on edge a week or so before he died. I chalked it up to the budget. The museum gets very little state or Federal funding. We rely mostly on donations, fundraisers, and sales from the gift shop."

"Now tell me about the skull."

"I honestly don't know that much about it. But I'll tell you what I do know. The skull was found in an ancient Mayan ruin about ten years ago by an archeologist named Rubin Fleming. It remained in his private collection until his death three years ago. Upon his death, it virtually disappeared. About a month ago my father said that he'd purchased it for the museum. I have no idea who he bought it from."

"There has to have been some kind of paperwork with it, wouldn't you think?" I asked.

"If there is, I haven't found it. Of course, I haven't really looked for it either. I wasn't even aware that my father took possession of the skull until you showed me the letter he wrote to Phoebe. Now that I know, Ill look for it."

"Please do, and contact me if you find it." I said, fishing a business card out of my bag and sliding it across the desk to Paul.

"I will."

"So why is this skull worth killing over? There must be others in existence."

"I have no idea. Maybe there's something unique about this one, something different than the others," he offered.

"Could be."

"Do you know where the skull is? Or if Madame Phoebe ever received it?" he asked.

"No I don't," I lied.

"I'd like to hire you to find the skull." he said decisively.

"I'm sorry, but I've already been retained by the Mt. Clements Police Department to assist in the murder of Madame Phoebe. It would be unethical of me to get paid by two different parties."

"I see," he said, somewhat disappointed.

"Thank you for your time, Paul." I said, rising from my chair.

"Thank you. I'll be in touch," he said leading me to the door of his office.

"I look forward to it," I said, shaking his hand. "Don't bother to see me out. I can find my way."

I left the museum and got back to my Jeep. Paul Friedman was lying. Now I needed to find out why.

Chapter Seven

Since I was already in Mt. Clements, I called Amy and arranged for her to meet me at Madame Phoebe's condominium. I wanted to take a look around. She readily agreed, and gave me directions.

Ten minutes later I pulled into the parking lot of a well-maintained complex. After a couple of tries, I found Madame Phoebe's address. Amy sat in her car waiting for me.

"Hi, Savannah," she said glumly as she led the way up the short walk to the front door.

"Hi Amy. How're you doing?"

"Okay. The funeral is tomorrow morning. You're coming aren't you?"

"Yes. I definitely plan to be there."

"Good," she said, inserting the key into the front door.

Amy stood back and allowed me to enter. When I walked into the foyer, I let out a sharp gasp. The entire place was ransacked.

Amy stood in the entranceway, her mouth agape.

"Oh my God," she finally gasped.

"Don't touch anything," I ordered as I reached into my bag for my cell phone.

I quickly dialed the Mt. Clements Police Department and asked for Detective Wilder.

I told him what happened and he said a crime scene team would be right there.

I ushered Amy out of Madame Phoebe's and out to her car.

"Go home," I ordered sharply.

"Shouldn't I wait for the police?" she asked, finally coming out of her daze.

"I'll do it," I snapped.

Amy obediently started her car and pulled out of the parking lot. A few minutes later, I saw Detective Wilder, followed by a crime scene unit pull into the parking lot.

"What happened?" he asked as we entered Madame Phoebe's townhouse.

"I met Amy Conterri here and when we walked through the door this is how we found the place."

"Where's Ms. Conterri now?"

"I sent her home. She appeared to be pretty shaken."

"This must have just happened last night. I was here with Ms. Conterri yesterday and the place was spotless," Detective Wilder said.

"Really. Find anything interesting?"

"I'm not sure. It would help if I knew what I was looking for," he said in frustration.

"Maybe this will help," I answered, pulling the letter from Arthur Friedman to Phoebe out of my bag and handing it to him.

"Where did you get this?" He asked.

"I found it in Madame Phoebe's papers. I planned on dropping a copy off to you this afternoon."

"Who's this DePaulo guy? What skull? Didn't Arthur Friedman die in a car accident a couple of weeks ago?" Detective Wilder was firing off questions so fast I didn't have time to answer.

"To answer your questions, DePaulo is an arts and antiquities dealer, the skull is from an ancient Mayan ruin, and yes, Arthur Friedman died in an apparent car accident."

"How'd you find out about the skull?" he asked as we watched the crime scene unit begin to process the scene.

55

"I went to the Museum of Ancient History this morning and had a talk with Arthur Friedman's son, Paul," I answered.

"What else did Paul Friedman say?"

"Nothing of much use I'm afraid. But I will tell you this. He was lying through his teeth. I just don't know why," I mused.

"I think I'm going to have a little chat with Mr. Friedman myself," he said with determination.

"Good luck."

"So, do you think DePaulo has the skull?" he asked.

"No. I'm pretty sure he doesn't," I answered. I hated not being able to tell Detective Wilder that I had the skull, but the less people who knew the better.

"Listen, I'm going to go make some phone calls from my car while the team is working. Are you going to stick around?" Detective Wilder asked.

"Yes. I want to have a look around if that's alright?"

"No problem," he said pulling his cell phone out of his jacket pocket.

I got a pair of latex gloves from one of the technicians and slowly began to work my way around the small living room. The beige sofa had been upended and the bottom liner had been slit. The matching recliner had suffered the same treatment.

Skirting my way around the evidence techs, I walked into the kitchen. The cabinets had been thoroughly searched as well as the small half bath off the kitchen area.

I worked my way back to the entranceway and went upstairs to the bedrooms. Madame

Phoebe's bedroom had beautiful hardwood floors and a large four-poster oak bed stood against the far wall and rested on an oriental rug in various colors of green and gold. The mattresses sat slit open and searched. The dresser and nightstands that matched the bed also were emptied and searched.

The second bedroom upstairs held a small desk and a computer. The drawers to the desk were empty and the contents strewn around the room. A thorough search would not be possible until the evidence techs had finished their job, but I could just about bet they wouldn't find anything.

I peeked in the master bath and found that it too had suffered the same treatment as the rest of the townhouse.

I walked back downstairs and found Detective Wilder talking to one of the evidence techs.

"Find anything?" he asked as I walked into the living room.

"Not yet. But I don't want to disturb anything until your team gets finished. Do we have a point of entry?"

"There's no sign of forced entry anywhere. So whoever did this either used a key or a lock picking kit," he answered.

"DePaulo," I quipped.

"More than likely. But we're going to keep working."

"Okay. I'm going. Not much I can do here until your team is finished. See you later," I said, heading for the front door.

"Keep in touch. I'll make a copy of this letter from Arthur Friedman, I'll give it to you at the funeral tomorrow," Detective Wilder said.

"Okay. Bye," I answered and headed out to my Jeep. I wanted to get back to my office. I had a lot of serious thinking to do.

When I got back to my office I made notes on my conversation with Paul Friedman and the break-in at Phoebe's townhouse. Then I poured a cup of coffee, lit a cigarette, and sat back to think.

After about an hour I came to some very disturbing conclusions. First, Amy Conterri was keeping something from me. Second, Paul Friedman was lying. This was going to put me in a very difficult situation with Sandra. Third, DePaulo was desperate to get his hands on that skull. I just hoped and prayed no one found out I had it tucked away in my safe at home. Fourth, I had to find out more about that skull.

I decided to tackle the problem of DePaulo first. I poured another cup of coffee and dialed Clint Mayfield's number. Clint is an old friend of mine in the FBI and proved invaluable in some of my other cases.

"FBI. Clint Mayfield," he answered in his slow Southern drawl.

"Hi Clint. It's Savannah," I said smiling at the sound of his voice.

"Hey darlin. How ya doing?"

"Doing great. How about yourself?"

"Fine. What's up?"

"Listen, can you run the name DePaulo through your magic computer and see what it spits out?"

"DePaulo. Capital D and capital P right?" he asked as I heard him punch some keys on his computer.

"Right."

"Got it. This is going to take awhile. I have to finish up a couple things. Can I e-mail you the results later today or first thing in the morning?"

"Sure no problem. Thanks, Clint."

"Anything for you darlin. Need anything else?"

"Yes, as a matter of fact I do. Have you ever heard of a FBI agent with the last name of Hathaway? Not Jackson Hathaway, but his father. Sorry but I don't know his first name?"

"Ahh, Special Agent Lincoln Hathaway," he said.

"So you knew him?"

"No, but I knew of him. He was real high up in the bureau. Some say he was next in line for the top position, but he died of a heart attack about nine years ago."

"Really? Wonder why I never heard of him?" I asked.

"Oh, he was before your time, darlin. But one heck of an agent from what I heard."

"So he made a lot of money?" I asked.

"Now that's a strange question, but yes, he did. At his level he was probably making seven digits. From what I understand he was some kind of financial genius."

"Wow. I see," I said quietly.

"Okay, I'll bite, why the questions?" he said laughing.

"I just hired his widow as my housekeeper and I'm dating his son, Jackson," I said with a chuckle.

"Okay. Gotcha. Talk to ya later darlin. Stay safe."

"You too. Bye," I said and hung up the phone.

Now all I had to do was wait. Something I'm not very good at. I decided to lock up the office and head home. I wanted to take another look at that skull.

I arrived home to find that Sandra and Lilly still weren't back from their shopping trip. I poured a glass of wine and headed into my den. After opening the blinds I went up the stairs to retrieve the skull from my safe.

I sat the box containing the skull on my desk and carefully unpacked it. The sunlight streaming through the front windows refracted off the skull, sending prisms of light dancing around the walls of my den.

In an eerie kind of way, the skull was beautiful. I couldn't help but admire the craftsmanship and skill that went into its creation.

I picked it up and examined it closely. I didn't see anything particularly exceptional or out of place on the skull, except for a small hole carved into the bottom. The hole was perfectly round and about an inch deep. I used a magnifying glass to examine every inch of the skull and discovered a minuscule crease running up the center. It started at the center of the hole in the bottom of the skull, ran all the way over the top, down the center of the nose and mouth, and ended back at the small hole at the bottom. So, either the skull was made in two pieces and put together, or it opened.

The hole at the bottom of the skull would indicate that at one time it sat on some type of base, or simply there as part of the creation process. Either way, it's an interesting discovery.

I picked up the skull and started to walk over to the window to look at it in the bright light. That's when I noticed it; a black Grand Am parked across the street from my house. There appeared to be two men in the car and the driver was using a pair of binoculars to peer into the front window of my den.

I quickly sat the skull down on the floor, ran and got my gun out of my bag, and raced through the front door. Just as I got down the front porch steps the car roared away. It sped around the corner before I could make out the license plate.

Totally dejected, I trudged through the freshly fallen snow back into the house.

For the first time in a long time I was scared. Someone knew I had the skull and they were willing to kill for it.

Chapter Eight

I closed the blinds in my den and picked the skull up off the floor. After repacking it in the box, I loaded it into the back of my Jeep and headed to my office. Taking mainly side streets to ensure no one followed me.

I arrived at my office and put the skull in the safe. I'd just closed the safe door when the telephone rang. I recoiled away from it like it was a snake ready to strike.

"Get a grip, Savannah," I chastised myself and reached for the phone.

"Savannah Williams," I said as casually as my voice would allow.

"Hi Savannah, its Sandra." I heard her breathe into the phone.

"Sandra. Where are you? Is Lilly still with you?" I asked urgently.

"We're just leaving the mall. What's wrong? You're wound tighter than a drum?" she asked with concern.

"Take Lilly out to dinner. In fact, take her to dinner and a movie then take her to your place for the night. Under no circumstances are you to bring her back to the house. Understand?" I said firmly.

"Whoa, what's up, Savannah? I know that tone. You're scared to death. What happened?"

"Just do as I say. Please," I pleaded, ignoring her questions.

"Hang on, let me tell Lilly," she sighed.

"Okay," I said, peeking out the front windows of my office through the blinds looking for any sign of the black Grand Am.

"Savannah. This is Lilly. We're on our way home. Meet us there. I'm calling Jackson and having him meet us," Lilly said sharply.

"No Lilly! Don't go home. Please. Go with Sandra. Don't fight me on this Lilly!" I said, my voice taking on a dangerous tone.

"Savannah, I don't know what happened to get you so worked up, but nothing is making me leave my house. Besides, you're upset dear, you shouldn't be alone," Lilly answered, ignoring me.

"No! I mean it Lilly! Don't go to the house!" I yelled.

"Savannah. Calm down. We'll be home in ten minutes. I'm going to let Lilly pick up a couple of things then I'll take her to my place," Sandra said.

"Sandra, if you see a black Grand Am, or any other car parked by my house, keep driving do you understand? I'll be home in five minutes," I said urgently.

"I understand. I have to go. Lilly wants to call Jackson. We'll be careful," She said quietly and the line went dead.

I quickly locked up my office, set the alarm, and raced down the stairs to my Jeep. I made it home in five minutes flat.

There was no sign of the Grand Am, but I kept a vigilant watch until I saw Sandra's BMW pull into the driveway.

Lilly and Sandra came through the front door laden with packages from their shopping trip.

"Now just what in the hell is going on?" Lilly demanded as she sat the packages on the stairs.

"I'd be interested to hear this myself," Jackson said as he walked through the front door. I hadn't even seen his truck pull into the driveway.

"Look," I said, wheeling around to face them. "Someone knows I have the skull. It isn't safe for you to be here, Lilly. You have to stay with Sandra or Jackson until this thing is over."

"I'm not going anywhere. Just calm yourself down. I've been through much worse than this with Jackson's father. I can take care of myself," Lilly said emphatically.

"Jackson," I pleaded looking at him for help.

"Where's the skull now?" Jackson asked.

"Locked in my safe at the office," I answered.

"Good. Mom, please do what Savannah asks. Just for tonight. You can stay with Sandra or me. Okay?" Jackson said.

"Well, just for tonight. But I'm coming back tomorrow, Lilly said firmly.

"Okay. Look. I'll bring you home in the morning after the funeral. Okay?" Jackson asked.

"Well. Okay," Lilly relented. "Just let me pack an overnight bag."

I breathed a sigh of relief as Lilly headed upstairs to pack.

"Now tell me what happened," Jackson said urgently as he led me into the den followed closely by Sandra.

"Madame Phoebe's funeral is tomorrow morning. I plan on going," I said as I finished recounting the events of the day.

"What time?"

"Ten."

"I'm going too," Jackson and Sandra said in unison.

"Okay."

"I'm ready. Why haven't you packed, Savannah?" Lilly said as she reappeared in the den with an overnight bag in her hand.

"Packed for what? I'm not going anywhere," I answered, confused.

"Well, you're not staying here. You haven't even had dinner yet. Plus, you said yourself its too dangerous," Lilly explained.

"Lilly, I meant it's too dangerous for you. I'll be fine. As for dinner, Sandra and I will go grab something."

"Well if you insist. Come on Jackson. I have to get ready for tomorrow," Lilly said.

"Be careful," Jackson whispered in my ear as he hugged and kissed me good-bye.

"I will."

Sandra and I waited until Jackson had Lilly safely ensconced in his truck and had drove away before we headed out to dinner.

"So how did your meeting go with Paul Friedman?" Sandra asked after we were settled into a private booth and ordered a bottle of wine at the Fisherman's Grill.

"Okay."

The waitress returned and poured our wine.

"Something's up. What is it, Savannah?" Sandra asked as she took her first sip of wine.

"Sandra, Paul lied to me today. I'm sure of it."

"About what? I've never known Paul to lie."

"About everything. Maybe lied isn't the right word, but he didn't tell the whole truth. How well do you really know Paul?" I answered, lighting a cigarette and taking a long sip of my wine.

"I'd say I know him pretty well," she bristled.

"Sandra, I'm sorry. Tell me about Arthur Friedman?" I asked, quickly changing the subject.

"Well, Arthur Friedman was somewhat of a control freak. I found him to be pleasant enough, but he had to have final say on everything. He was a very private person," she answered.

"How was the relationship between Paul and his father?" I asked as the waitress delivered our salads.

"I honestly have to say not very good. Paul was the assistant curator, but really only in charge of the exhibits. His father wouldn't let him have any of the responsibility for acquisitions or the business end of the museum. Paul basically handled the day to day operation of the museum, but that's about it."

"So, did Paul resent his father?"

"Yes. I suppose he did. But I'm not sure it wasn't frustration more than resentment. Paul had so many great ideas on how to improve the museum, but Arthur didn't want to hear it. All the marketing and public relations work I do for the museum is very conservative. Although I expect that will change now that Paul is in charge," she answered between bites of her salad.

"I see. So how did Paul handle the news of his father's death?" I asked as I put aside my salad plate and lit another cigarette.

"He was naturally upset, but I think he felt that he had to be strong for his mother. So I think he hid most of his grief. As bad as their relationship was, I think Paul truly loved his father," she replied, after pausing to think for a minute.

"I'm sure he did."

The waitress brought our dinners, and we spent the next few minutes eating.

"Did Paul or his father ever mention anyone by the name of DePaulo?" I asked casually after we had finished and ordered another bottle of wine.

"No, not that I remember. Why?"

"His name keeps popping up in this case."

"Do you think this DePaulo guy had something to do with Madame Phoebe's death?"

"I'm not sure, but it's possible," I answered, pouring Sandra and myself another glass of wine.

"Okay, you've been plying me with questions all during dinner. Now it's my turn. What skull were you talking about when we got to the house tonight?"

"Okay, but this is between you and me. Got it," I said seriously.

"Okay. Go on," she said, her emerald eyes gleaming.

"I received a skull made out of some type of crystal from Madame Phoebe the day after she was murdered. My theory is that she was murdered for the skull."

"So that's why you were so panicked tonight. Someone knows you have it."

"Exactly, but not a word to anyone, especially Paul. Understand?" I said firmly.

"I understand. But where did Madame Phoebe get the skull?"

"From Arthur Friedman."

"Oh my God. So that could mean that Arthur's death..." Her voice trailed off, as the reality of the situation hit her.

"Exactly. Now hush," I hissed as the waitress approached with our check.

I paid the check with my credit card while Sandra poured more wine into our glasses.

"So what's your next move?" she asked, after draining her glass of wine in two gulps and poured herself another.

"I have to track the history of the skull. There has to be something about that skull that makes it worth killing for. Paul said he would look for the paperwork that had to have come with it and that he would call me if he found it."

"But you don't think he will."

"No, I really don't."

"He might surprise you."

"Yes, he might at that," I agreed as I sat my napkin on the table and slid into my coat.

"Ready?" I asked Sandra.

"Yes. Let's go," she said, rising from the table to put on her coat.

When we'd arrived at the restaurant, we'd parked behind my office and walked the short distance through town to the restaurant.

We chatted about the purchases Lilly made today as we walked. We'd just crossed the street to go to my office when I heard a powerful engine roar to life and the squeal of tires. I quickly reached into my bag to pull out my gun, but it was too late. I caught just a glimpse of the black Grand Am illuminated by one of the streetlights before I heard the sound of gunshots.

"Get down!" I screamed pushing Sandra to the ground behind a parked car and shielding her with my body.

The car was going so fast one of the occupants only had time to squeeze off two or three shots before it sped out of site and around the corner.

"Are you okay?" I whispered to Sandra as I got to my knees and peered up over the hood of the parked car.

"Yes. Savannah! They tried to kill us!" Sandra screamed hysterically.

"No, they didn't try to kill us. They had us dead to rights when we were crossing the street. That was just a warning," I said tensely, putting my arms around Sandra's shaking body to calm her down.

"Come on. We have to move," I said urgently, helping her to her feet.

I cautiously led Sandra to my Jeep, keeping her behind me, and my gun at the ready. I took the long way home, careful not to be followed. Not that it mattered. They already knew where I lived.

"Come home with me tonight," Sandra pleaded as we pulled into the garage.

"No. I'll be fine. They won't be back tonight."

"Are you sure?"

"Positive. Now go home," I said with more confidence then I felt.

"Okay, but promise me you'll be careful," she begged, giving me a hug good night.

"I will. Night."

Once I had Sandra safely in her BMW and on her way home, I checked to make sure the house was secure. I set the alarm and settled in on the couch with my gun and a blanket.

Chapter Nine

I woke up about six, stiff and sore from sleeping on the couch. I fed the dogs and hunted down Max to give him breakfast.

Donning the only black dress I owned, I wandered into the kitchen to make coffee. It took me forever to find everything. Lilly had rearranged the kitchen to her liking and by the time I'd found the coffee filters and coffee, I was grumpy and irritable.

I'd just poured my first cup of coffee when the phone rang. I viciously grabbed it out of its cradle and hit the talk button.

"What!" I barked into the phone.

"Good morning to you too, Savannah," Jackson said chuckling.

"Oh hi. Sorry," I said in a more normal tone of voice.

"Everything okay?"

"Other than Sandra and I being shot at last night, and my being sore from sleeping on the couch, everything's just fine," I snapped.

"What! Did you call the police?" he said aghast.

"No. Of course not."

"Why in the hell not? Savannah!" he screamed into the phone.

"Because I wasn't in the mood to explain everything to them. Besides, if they had wanted to kill us they could have. It was just a warning."

"A warning from who? DePaulo?"

"Probably. But I don't know for sure."

"Damn it, Savannah. I'm on my way over there. Stay put," he ordered.

"To do what? Ride in like a knight on a white horse and save the damsel in distress? No thank you. I'm not in distress and am perfectly capable of taking care of myself," I snapped.

"You know what? You're right. You want to be like this? Have at it. I'm not in the mood for it."

"Fine," I said emphatically.

"Fine. See you at the funeral," he said.

"Don't force yourself," I retorted and slammed down the phone.

"Men!" I screamed at Max sitting on the kitchen counter calmly watching me with his big gold eyes.

Max walked up to me and I spent a minute or two stroking his soft, black fur. When he'd had enough, he jumped down from the counter and sauntered into the great room to take a nap.

I stomped into my bathroom to finish getting ready for Madame Phoebe's funeral.

In the middle of drying my hair I heard the dogs barking wildly in the other room. I ran out of the bathroom and down the hall to the front door. The doorbell was pealing loudly.

Thinking it was Jackson, I yanked open the door to find three men standing there. I thought I recognized two of them from the black Grand Am, but I couldn't be sure. They were both very tall, and very well put together.

The third man appeared to be of Italian descent. He stood about five foot nine and had a medium build. I judged him to be in his mid to late forties. His dark, almost black eyes were darting from me to the dogs whose barks had become low throaty growls. He had a well-trimmed mustache and was dressed in a black suit, black shirt, and black and yellow tie. A black wool cape rested lightly on his shoulders. A mixture of adrenaline and fear shot through my body.

"Savannah Williams?" The man asked in clipped English. I detected a slight European accent.

"Yes," I said tentatively. I was scared. The only thing that stood between them and me was the dogs and a storm door. My gun was in the bedroom.

"My name is DePaulo. May I come in? I believe we need to talk," he asked politely.

"If your friends wait outside," I answered, motioning to his two apparent bodyguards.

"Agreed, if your dogs do the same," he said with a slight bow.

"Agreed. Wait a second," I said, closing the door and locking it.

I let the dogs out into the backyard and ran to get my gun, but realized I had no place to hide it. I ended up sticking it in the drawer of my desk in the den for easy reach.

I walked to the front door and opened it. DePaulo stood on the porch alone. I saw the two other men waiting in the front seat of a big, black Lincoln.

"Please come in," I said, stepping aside to allow him to enter.

"Thank you," he said gallantly and walked into the house, looking around for the dogs.

"Would you care for a cup of coffee? It's fresh," I asked awkwardly.

"Yes, thank you. Black, please," he answered.

I walked into the kitchen with DePaulo close on my heels. I poured us each a cup of coffee and handed him his.

"Why don't we talk in the den? We'll be more comfortable there," I suggested.

"As you wish," he answered and stepped aside politely to allow me to lead him to the den. I felt uncomfortable with him behind me, but I didn't see that I had a choice.

I settled in my desk chair and DePaulo made himself comfortable in one of the overstuffed guest chairs.

"What can I do for you, Mr. DePaulo?" I asked, taking a sip of coffee while trying to keep my hands from shaking.

"I will get right to the point, Ms. Williams. It has come to my attention that you are in possession of a certain crystal skull. I have great interest in that skull and I'm here to make a deal," he said in a very businesslike manner.

"What kind of a deal? The kind you tried to make last night when your friends shot at me? I don't take too kindly to being shot at, Mr. DePaulo."

"An unfortunate error in judgment on their part. I can assure you it won't happen again. I'm not prone to violence."

I almost believed him.

"Really. I find that interesting," I said with a slight sarcastic note to my voice.

"To get back to the deal I spoke of. I'm prepared to offer you half a million dollars for the skull," he said, not blinking an eye.

"Mr. DePaulo, that's quite a generous offer. However, I must respectfully decline at this time," I responded with equal detachment.

"For what reason?" he asked, taking a sip of his coffee.

"For several reasons actually. For one, the skull is involved in a murder investigation.

73

Second, a dear friend who was recently murdered entrusted the safety of that skull to me. Third, until I know who murdered my friend and they are behind bars, the skull is going to stay safely hidden away. I don't even know you? Why would I give you the skull?" I challenged him.

"All that you say is true I'm sure. I'm sorry for the loss of your dear friend. My condolences. You are a very smart woman, Ms. Williams. I have assembled quite an impressive dossier on you and respect your talents and abilities. You're right. You don't know me. Allow me to tell you about myself. I am a dealer in relics and antiquities. I acquire certain items for a very elite clientele. I have been hired to secure the crystal skull in your possession for a particular client," he said, looking me square in the eye.

"Why this skull? What's so special about it?" I asked curiously. Damn he was good.

"That I do not know. My client only gave me these instructions. May I?" He asked, opening the front of his black wool coat to reveal a piece of paper sticking out of an inner pocket.

"Please," I answered, seeing no sign of a shoulder holster or gun.

He withdrew a piece of folded plain white paper and handed it to me. Typed neatly on the paper was the following:

DePaulo,

>Please acquire a particular crystal skull. The skull is of Mayan origin. It was once in the possession of archeologist, Rubin Fleming. Before his death three years ago, the skull fell into the hands of a man named Thomas Markley, a jeweler and art dealer. Mr. Markley met with an

untimely death and the skull has disappeared. You will know you have the right skull if there is a small hole in the bottom of the skull. I will pay whatever it takes to get my hands on that skull.

The signature had been blacked out with a magic marker. I refolded the paper and handed it back to DePaulo.

"Comments, Ms. Williams?" he asked.

"I sympathize with your situation Mr. DePaulo, but I still can't sell you the skull. It's not mine to sell. Someone, who shall remain nameless, purchased the skull. When they purchased it, they sent it to my friend who sent it to me for safekeeping the day before her murder. When this whole matter is resolved to my satisfaction, perhaps you can work out a deal with the owner of the skull," I said kindly.

"Ah, I am disappointed, but I understand. I will be in touch, Ms. Williams. In the meantime, I assure you that my men will leave you alone," he said, rising from his chair.

"Thank you," I said, walking him to the door.

"It's been a pleasure. I shall look forward to our future meetings, Ms. Williams," he said, taking my hand and kissing it.

"As shall I," I said, gently withdrawing my hand.

I watched as DePaulo walked back to his car and got into the backseat. I watched as they slowly backed out of the driveway and drove down the road.

With a sigh of relief, I locked the door and let the dogs back in the house.

If DePaulo was telling the truth, which is highly suspect, this put a whole new light on the case. Racing back in to my office, I quickly copied down what I could remember of the letter that DePaulo showed me.

I went into the kitchen, and after a short search, found a plastic zip lock bag. I folded the bag inside out and placed it carefully over the coffee cup DePaulo had used. Then I folded the cup into the bag and zipped it shut. After placing the cup in my bag, I set the alarm and headed for the funeral.

At exactly ten o'clock I pulled into the parking lot of the funeral home. After finding a place to park, I raced through the door and took a seat at the back.

Jackson, Lilly, and Sandra were all there and I got a trio of dirty looks for being late. Sitting next to Sandra was Paul Friedman.

The service was short, but nice. Amy sat in the front row, dry eyed, but somber.

After the service, Jackson, Lilly, Paul Friedman, and Sandra made their way over to me.

"Where were you?" Lilly demanded sternly.

"I had a little visitor before I left the house. Sorry," I answered meekly.

"Who?" Jackson asked.

"DePaulo," I answered flatly.

"Are you okay?" Sandra asked with concern.

"Oh, I'm fine. Jackson, I need you to take this cup and run the prints for me please," I asked politely as I fished the plastic bag with DePaulo's coffee cup out of my bag.

"DePaulo's?" Jackson asked, putting the cup discreetly in his coat pocket.

"Yes,"

There was to be a small reception at the Fisherman's Grill after the service and I sent all of them ahead. I wanted to talk to Amy.

"Hi, how are you holding up?" I asked sympathetically.

"I'm doing okay. I'm still so upset about the break in at Phoebe's house."

"Yes. I'm sure you are," I answered. "Amy, I need you to think. Did Phoebe ever mention anything about a crystal skull or someone by the name of DePaulo?"

"I never heard her mention the name DePaulo, but I remember her talking about a crystal skull. Why?"

"I think Phoebe was murdered by someone desperate to get their hands on that skull. DePaulo is a relic and antiquities dealer. His name has come up a few times."

"What does the skull have to do with Phoebe's death?

"Phoebe had the skull before she died. A friend gave it to her for safekeeping."

"Phoebe had the skull?" she exclaimed.

"Yes."

"So you think this DePaulo person killed Phoebe to get the skull?"

"I honestly can't say. It's too early in the investigation. What did Phoebe say about the skull?"

"She said that a friend of hers had just acquired a very special crystal skull. Phoebe was quite anxious to see it. She believed that crystal skulls held mystical powers. You know how she was," she said, rolling her eyes.

"What else did she say about it?" I asked, ignoring Amy's last remark.

77

"Not much really. She said the skull was Mayan. That's about it. What happened to the skull then? Did her killer get it?"

"No. Phoebe sent the skull to someone to keep it safe."

"Who?" Amy asked.

"I can't say. But the skull is safe," I answered evasively.

"Are you coming to the reception?" she asked, briskly changing the subject.

"Yes. I'll be there shortly."

"Okay. See you there then," she said, and went to gather her coat and bag.

After Amy left I found myself alone with Madame Phoebe. I walked up to the casket and gazed down at the once lovely woman lying so still.

"Phoebe. I will find who did this to you. I promise," I whispered as I stroked her hair.

I swear I heard her answer, "I know you will, Savannah."

With a heavy heart, I left the funeral home to walk the short distance to the Fisherman's Grill.

"Something's really wrong with this whole case. I'm missing something important. I just have to figure out what it is," I thought to myself as I walked down Washington towards the Fisherman's Grill.

Chapter Ten

When I got to the restaurant I found Sandra, Jackson, Lilly, and Paul Friedman sitting at a table in the back.

"Hi, Savannah." They said in unison as I joined them at the table.

"Hi," I said sadly, allowing Jackson to seat me and pour me a glass of wine.

I glanced around the restaurant and saw Detective Wilder sitting at the bar scanning the group of mourners.

"Excuse me for a second," I said to the others and got up to go talk to him.

"I had an interesting visitor this morning," I said after we exchanged greetings.

"Oh yeah? Who?" he asked.

"DePaulo."

"What!" he exclaimed, and then lowered his voice to just above a whisper. "What happened?"

I quickly summarized the meeting between DePaulo and myself for Detective Wilder.

"Wow. Do you believe him?"

"Almost, but not quite. It still doesn't explain why his men shot at me the other night."

"You were shot at?"

"Yes, just a warning though. They had a clear shot when my friend and I were walking across the street."

"Interesting. Oh, I stopped by the museum and talked to Paul Friedman yesterday."

"Oh?" I answered.

"I agree with you. He's not telling all he knows."

"I wonder what he's hiding?" I said.

"I don't know, but it'll come out eventually, it always does. Oh, I have something for you," he said reaching into his jacket pocket and pulling out the copy of the letter Arthur Friedman had sent to Phoebe.

"Thanks. Keep your eyes open. I have to go," I said.

"You too. Keep in touch."

I rejoined the others at the table and put the letter Detective Wilder gave me in my bag.

"What was that about?" Paul asked.

"Just touching base. Why? Do you know Detective Wilder?" I asked, my eyes narrowing.

"He stopped by the museum yesterday to talk to me. I didn't realize you two knew each other," Paul said, meeting my gaze.

"Why don't we go get our food, the buffet is open," Sandra said, trying to take the tension out of the air.

"Yes, lets," Paul answered and rose from the table.

"That's a man with a secret," Lilly said, as she watched Paul and Sandra walk to the buffet.

"Why do you say that, Lilly?" I asked curiously.

"He's very defensive," she mused.

"Yes he is," I agreed.

"I'm hungry. Lets get our food," Jackson said, changing the subject.

We all got our food and met back at the table. Jackson poured me another glass of wine and the conversation turned to general small talk while we ate.

I really wasn't very hungry, and just moved my food around on the plate. After about ten minutes, I felt restless, so I left the table to go to the ladies room.

I sat in the ladies room on a small settee to have a cigarette and think. After about five minutes, I gathered up my bag and headed out to rejoin the others.

Paul Friedman stood waiting for me outside the bathroom door.

"I didn't think you'd ever come out," he said with a slight smile.

"What do you want, Paul?" I asked impatiently.

"I have a present for you," he replied as he reached into his suit coat pocket.

"Oh? What's that?"

"I found the paperwork for the skull. I'm afraid it's a bit sketchy, but you're welcome to look at it. I made you a copy," He answered handing me a sealed envelope.

"Thanks," I said, tucking the papers into my bag.

I walked around Paul to head back to the table when he reached out and grabbed my arm.

"What is it with you anyway?" he asked, his eyes blazing.

"What about me?" I asked, my eyes flashing as they met his.

"Ever since we met you have shown nothing but animosity towards me. Are you threatened by me dating Sandra or what?" he said, holding my gaze.

"Don't flatter yourself," I snapped, yanking my arm out of his grasp.

"Well then what is it?" he hissed back.

"You really want to know? Okay. Here goes. I hate being lied to, and you lied to me when we met at the museum," I retorted.

"I didn't lie to you," he whined.

"Okay, but you didn't tell me the whole truth. You have a secret Paul, and I'm going to find out what it is. Of course you could save us both a lot of time and trouble and tell me now," I said, my eyes narrowing.

Paul didn't say a word.

"I didn't think so. But if I find out that you have lied to Sandra, or put her in any danger, I will come after you," I said, my voice low and dangerous.

"Are you threatening me, Ms. Williams?" he asked, raising an eyebrow.

"Not at all, Mr. Friedman." I said as I walked away from him to rejoin the others at the table.

"Did you see Paul? He left for the restroom shortly after you did," Sandra said, gazing toward the restrooms.

"We chatted in the hallway. I'm sure he'll be right back," I answered, taking a sip of wine.

"What did you say to him, Savannah?" Sandra asked angrily.

"Nothing I didn't deserve to hear," Paul said as he gave Sandra a kiss on the cheek and sat down.

"Sorry, but I have work to do," I said, rising from the table and gathering my things and walking out of the restaurant.

I was almost to my Jeep when Detective Wilder caught up with me.

"Are you okay?" He said as he fell in stride with me.

"I'm fine. Why, Detective?" I said as I walked.

"I saw you and Paul Friedman having a discussion outside the bathroom. What was all that about? And please, call me Brent," he said.

"He gave me a copy of the paperwork for the skull," I answered.

"Really? Have you looked at it yet?"

"No, I'm going to when I get home though. Care to join me?" I asked with a wicked smile unlocking the door to my truck.

"With pleasure. I'll follow you."

"Okay." I answered.

I pulled out of my parking place and saw Detective Wilder getting into a dark blue Dodge Dakota a few spaces away from me. He fell in behind me, and a few minutes we pulled into my driveway.

After retrieving a beer for Detective Wilder and a glass of wine for myself we headed into my den.

I slit the envelope open and pulled out two sheets of folded paper.

One of the papers said Certificate of Authenticity; the other a Bill of Sale from a woman named Nancy Webster to Arthur Friedman on behalf of the Museum of Ancient History with a purchase price listed at two hundred thousand dollars.

"That's strange," I said looking over the documents.

"Yes, it is. Who's Nancy Webster?"

"No, not that. The Certificate of Authenticity, it's not right!" I exclaimed.

"What about it?"

"Not just that, but the ledger sheet that lists all the owners of the skull is missing," I answered, looking at Detective Wilder.

"Okay, I'm totally lost here. Explain." he said.

"Okay. First, the Certificate of Authenticity is strange because Rubin Fleming found the skull at a Mayan ruin. There would be no Certificate of Authenticity. The only way a Certificate of Authenticity could exist as far as the skull is concerned is if Rubin Fleming made one up to state that this skull is the one he found at the site and its approximate age. Second, all artifacts come with a type of ledger sheet that lists all the owners, that way it's possible to trace the history of the artifact," I explained.

"Okay. I'm with you so far, go on."

"This Certificate of Authenticity is signed by Nancy Webster, not Rubin Fleming. Now, it's possible that Nancy Webster had this one made up for the sale to Arthur Friedman, but it still seems strange," I mused.

"So, what you're saying is that this Nancy Webster would have no way of knowing if this is indeed the skull that was found at the Mayan site or not."

"Exactly."

"We need to find this Nancy Webster," he said.

"And, we need to find that ledger sheet," I added.

"Okay, I understand all that, but how is this going to help us find out who killed Madame Phoebe?" he said.

"Well, whoever killed Phoebe killed her for the skull. If we trace the skull, we find the killer. There is something about this skull that makes it special. Once we know what that something is, it'll make our job a lot easier. I don't know about you, but I have a list of suspects a mile long. The sooner I can start eliminating some of them the better," I explained.

"Agreed. Let's compare lists shall we?"

"Okay. But first, are we in agreement that Arthur Friedman's death wasn't an accident?" I asked.

"Yes. As a matter of fact, I had his car towed to one of the crime labs and a team is going over it as we speak. I also have the Medical Examiner running more tests on Arthur Friedman's tissue samples. I should have the results later this week," he answered.

"Excellent. Okay. My list of suspects includes Paul Friedman, DePaulo, this Nancy Webster, Amy Conterri, and the unknown client of DePaulo's. What's your list?" I asked.

"Same as yours. Oh, by the way, the Medical Examiner placed Madame Phoebe's time of death at somewhere between three and four that afternoon," he said.

"Did you ask Paul Friedman where he was during that time frame?"

"Yes. He said he was at the museum. I talked to some of the museum staff. His secretary was at lunch from one thirty to two thirty. She said when she got back from lunch he was in his office. The rest of the museum staff was busy setting up a new exhibit and knew they'd seen him, they just didn't remember what time."

"Okay. So he had motive and opportunity."

"Yes, but we have no idea where DePaulo or his men were during that time frame."

"True, but I have a feeling I'll have an opportunity to ask him about that," I chuckled.

"You like him don't you," he teased.

"Yes, in a way I do. He's very polite and disarming. He has a certain European charm," I admitted.

"Yeah, well don't let his charm fool you," he warned.

"Oh, I won't," I said.

Just then Sandra, Jackson and Lilly arrived at the house.

Lilly headed upstairs to change and Sandra and Jackson joined Detective Wilder and I in the den.

After exchanging greetings, Detective Wilder got up to leave.

"Keep in touch, Savannah. I have to get back to work." Detective Wilder said as he put on his coat.

"Okay. You too. See you later." I said, walking him to the door.

I let him out and locked the door behind him. Then I headed into my bedroom to change out of my dress and into a black sweat suit and tennis shoes.

I poured myself another glass of wine and headed back into the den. I made a few notes on the papers that Paul had given me and slid them into a file folder. I had a lot of work to do, but first I had to get rid of Sandra and Jackson.

"Paul told me he gave you the paperwork on the skull," Sandra said.

"Yes he did," I answered, lighting a cigarette.

"I told you he would," Sandra said rather defensively.

"Yes, and you were right. I'm sorry," I answered, trying to defuse her anger.

"Why don't you like him, Savannah? I so hoped you two would get along. I love him," she wailed.

"I never said I didn't like him, Sandra. But I don't trust him and I know he isn't being completely honest with me. I'm sorry, but that's how I feel," I explained.

"Paul is a very private person, just like his father. He'll come around," she said.

"I'm sure you're right."

"Anyway, I have to go. Paul wants me to come to the museum to talk about a more aggressive marketing campaign." Sandra said rising from her chair.

"Oh good. It's a beautiful museum," I said, trying to smooth her ruffled feathers.

"Yes it is. See you later. Bye," Sandra said with a wave of her hand as she let herself out of the house.

I breathed a big sigh of relief after Sandra left. I'd known her dating Paul was going to complicate things, I just hadn't realized how much until now.

"Nice job. She didn't believe a word you said," Jackson muttered as he took a long swig of his beer.

"Jackson, right now I could care less," I retorted.

"I got that impression."

"Listen, I don't mean to rush you, but I have a lot of work to do. Can we catch up with each other later?" I asked sweetly.

"Sure thing. Besides, I want to get that cup you gave me with DePaulo's fingerprints on it to the lab," he said rising to put on his coat.

"Great. Thanks," I answered, giving him a hug.

"No problem. But if I were you, I would call Sandra and make nice," he advised.

"I will," I sighed.

I walked Jackson to the door and after he left, returned to my den and shut myself in. Time to go to work.

Chapter Eleven

I'd just retrieved my case file from the safe when the phone rang. I scurried down the stairs to answer it, but it stopped ringing before I got halfway down.

A few seconds later, Lilly knocked on the door to the den.

"Come in," I said.

"Savannah dear, a man named Clint Mayfield is on the phone for you. Would you like me to take a message?" Lilly asked sweetly.

"No thanks. I'll take it," I answered, reaching for the phone.

"Hi Clint," I said cheerfully into the phone.

"Hi darlin. How goes the battle?"

"Good. What's up?" I asked, as I heard Lilly hang up the extension.

"Listen, I ran that DePaulo guy through the computer for you. I'm calling with the results," he answered.

"Great. Shoot," I said reaching for a pen and pad of paper.

"Viktor DePaulo, spelled with a "k", is his full name. The computer says he's a dealer in antiquities and ancient relics. He's been the subject of several investigations dealing with the sale of art and relics in the black market. There wasn't enough evidence for an indictment so the investigations were closed. His last known address is in Newport Beach, California. There's some other information in a different file, but it's going to take me a few days to get to it. I'm really busy," he said.

"Okay. No problem. Can you fax it to me?" I asked.

"Sure thing. It's on the way."

"Okay. Thanks, Clint. Talk to you later."

"Anything for you, Savannah. Stay safe," he said and hung up.

A couple of minutes later the fax machine came to life and the information on DePaulo began to come through.

After reading the information on DePaulo, I went to put it in the case file when the notes I'd made on the letter DePaulo had showed me caught my eye.

The letter had said that a man named Thomas Markley had met with an untimely death. To me, that's just a fancy way of saying murder. But first, I wanted to track down Rubin Fleming's family.

If I could find out what is so special about the skull, the real motive for murder would be revealed.

A quick search of the Internet revealed that Rubin Fleming, the archeologist that found the skull, had been a professor at a well-known university in Southern California.

After completing a little more research and making a few phone calls, I had what I needed. After formulating a quick plan, I placed a call to the university.

After being transferred two times, I finally ended up talking to a helpful secretary named Marissa in the Department of Archeology.

"Hello, Marissa, my name is Professor Leslie McPherson, is Professor Rubin Fleming available?" I asked.

"I'm sorry, Professor McPherson, but Professor Fleming passed away three years ago. Is there something I can help you with?" Marissa asked.

"Passed away! Oh my goodness! I didn't know. I've been out of the country on a dig," I explained.

"Yes. I'm sorry. Were you close to the Professor?" Marissa asked with concern.

"Yes. We were on the dig in Mexico together a few years ago," I explained.

"Oh, I'm so sorry. Is there anything I can do?" she inquired.

"I would love to be able to send my condolences, however belated, to his wife. Oh, what's her name?" I asked in frustration.

"You mean Eleanor?" she asked.

"Yes. Eleanor. How could I forget? She was always so gracious when I dined at their home, in oh, San Diego, wasn't it?" I said.

"San Vicente, just outside of San Diego. It's easy to get confused," Marissa thoughtfully corrected me.

"Oh, of course. Is Mrs. Fleming still there? I have her number around here somewhere I'm sure," I inquired, noisily shuffling some papers close to the phone.

"As far as I know. Hang on a second," she said.

"Blast it. One of these days I'll get organized," I muttered in response, still shuffling the papers.

"I looked for the number, but I guess its been deleted from our computer system. I'm sorry," she said.

"Oh no problem. I'm sure I'll find it. Thank you so much, Marissa. You have been so kind," I said.

"Oh, any time Professor. Have a good day," Marissa said cheerfully and rang off.

"Oh, I will, Marissa." I said, smiling smugly as I hung up the phone.

A quick search of the white pages on the Internet yielded an E. Fleming listed in San Vicente.

"Bingo," I said, writing down the number.

I glanced at the clock in my den. It was almost five here, so still early afternoon in California.

I opened the door to my den and found Lilly in the kitchen starting to prepare a light dinner.

"Lilly. I have an important phone call to make. Could you see that I'm not disturbed for a little while?" I asked, picking up a piece of carrot that Lilly was slicing for the salads.

"Of course dear. Dinner is in an hour. Jackson and Sandra are going to join us if that's okay," Lilly replied.

"It's fine," I answered and happily crunched on the carrot as I walked back to my den.

After closing the doors, I dialed Eleanor Fleming's phone number.

"Hello?" An older woman's voice said into the phone after the second ring.

"Hello. Is this Eleanor Fleming?" I asked kindly.

"Yes it is. Who is this please?"

"Mrs. Fleming, my name is Savannah Williams and I'm a private detective in Michigan. Do you have a few minutes?"

"A private detective. Why are you calling me?"

I spent a few minutes filling her in on the crystal skull, Arthur Friedman, and Madame Phoebe.

"Sounds like you have a tiger by the tail. How can I help you?" she commented when I had finished.

"What can you tell me about the crystal skull your husband found in the Mayan ruins in Mexico?"

"Not much really. He kept it as a memento from the dig. I never much cared for it, but he loved it so," she said wistfully.

"I see. What is it about that skull that makes it different from the others that have been found?"

"Why, nothing that I know of. Why? Have you noticed something about it?"

"Yes. There's a small hole on the bottom of the skull and it looks like it was made in two pieces and then put together."

"Now that's strange. There wasn't a hole in the bottom of the skull when Rubin had it."

"Are you sure?"

"I'm positive. Lord knows I dusted that blasted thing enough. If there'd been a hole in it, I'd have seen it. And I'm positive it was all one solid piece. Rubin was very fond of pointing out oddities in his finds. He would have surely pointed that out to me," she answered with a wry chuckle.

"I'm sure he would have. Now, when Professor Fleming died, what did you do with the skull?"

"Why nothing. Rubin gave it away to a dear friend before he died."

"Really? Why?"

"Rubin had cancer. He knew he was dying. He began to give some of his favorite things away to friends who'd admired them. He felt that they should be given to people who loved them as much as he did."

"I understand. Who did he give the skull to?"

"A good friend of his named Thomas Markley."

Interesting. Would you happen to have Mr. Markley's phone number?"

"Oh, Thomas is dead Ms. Williams, but his widow, Rebecca, and I still stay in contact. Hold on a minute, I'll get her number for you," she offered graciously.

"Thank you."

A minute or two later Eleanor returned to the phone and gave me Rebecca Markley's telephone number.

"Thank you. Just a couple of more questions if you don't mind," I said after writing down the phone number.

"Not at all, what else can I tell you?" she said eagerly.

I got the impression that Eleanor was a lonely woman and happy to have someone to talk to.

"Did your husband ever have a Certificate of Authenticity to go with the skull?"

"No, since he kept it in his private collection he didn't see the need."

"That makes sense. Would you happen to know how Thomas Markley died?"

"Oh, it was tragic really. You see Thomas and a few friends of his went hunting. There was a hunting accident and Thomas was accidentally shot by another hunter."

"How convenient," I said quietly.

"I'm sorry dear I didn't hear you?"

"I'm sorry, I said, how terrible," I replied, admonishing myself for being so careless.

"Yes it was."

"What did Mrs. Markley do with the skull after Mr. Markley's death?"

"Oh, I really don't know. We never spoke of it," she said thoughtfully.

"One last question, I promise," I said with a slight laugh.

"Oh, no problem, Ms. Williams. I enjoy talking to you," she said gaily.

"Thank you. Have you ever heard the name Viktor DePaulo?"

"Oh, that man is dangerous, Ms. Williams. Stay away from him!" she cautioned.

"Why do you say dangerous?"

"Well, perhaps dangerous isn't the right word. Scandalous is probably more appropriate. DePaulo is well known in the world of antiquities and relics, Ms. Williams. He would acquire certain items for his clients at a very large fee, and not always through legitimate means if you understand what I'm saying."

"Oh, I understand perfectly, Mrs. Fleming. Thank you for your time. I really must go," I said gratefully.

"Oh, call anytime dear. In fact, may I have your number? That way if I think of anything else, I can let you know. Oh, and let me know how this all works out won't you?"

"Of course."

After giving Eleanor Fleming my office phone number I rang off. Mrs. Fleming had sure given me a lot to think about and I quickly to make notes before I forgot anything.

Anxious to glean more information about the skull, I dialed Rebecca Markley's phone number.

"Hello?" An older, but energetic voice said into the phone.

"Hello. Mrs. Markley?" I asked.

"Yes," she said tentatively.

"Mrs. Markley, my name is Savannah Williams. I am a private detective in Michigan. Eleanor Fleming gave me your number. Do you have a few minutes?"

"Oh, Eleanor, how is she?"

"She's fine."

"That's good to hear. Now what can I do for you, Ms. Williams?"

I quickly explained the purpose of my call to Mrs. Markley.

"Oh that damn skull. I told Thomas it was nothing but trouble," she exclaimed.

"Well, apparently you were right," I agreed.

"I usually am about these things. Now what do you want to know?"

It was readily apparent that Mrs. Markley is a no nonsense kind of woman, so I decided to be direct.

"When your husband died, what happened to the skull?"

"Oh I sold it. I hated that thing," she replied.

"Sold it to who if I may ask."

"Hiram Webster."

"Who's Hiram Webster?"

"He was a business associate of my husbands."

"Is his wife's name Nancy by any chance?"

"Why, yes it is. Do you know Nancy?"

"No, I'm sorry I don't. Anyway, when your husband had the skull, was there a small hole on the bottom of it?"

"Not at first. But Thomas said that he dropped the darn thing and it split in half. He used jeweler's epoxy to put it back together. I guess when it fell a large chip came out of the bottom of the skull so Thomas made it into a hole so it wouldn't look damaged," she explained.

"I see. I'm sorry to have to bring this up, but could you tell me about Mr. Markley's hunting accident?"

"Oh, it's okay. I don't mind talking about it. Thomas, and two business acquaintances of his went hunting. Thomas wasn't wearing his orange hunting vest. Anyway, another hunter saw something move and shot at it. That something was Thomas."

"So one of Mr. Markley's business associates who shot him?"

"Yes, poor Scott felt just terrible. But it was Thomas' own fault for not wearing his vest."

"Were there charges filed?"

"Oh no. It was an accident."

"What's Scott's last name?"

"Scott Jacobs. He was Thomas' apprentice."

"Oh, so he worked in the jewelry store with Mr. Markley?"

"Yes. He'd only been there a short time. Thomas was very fond of him."

"Do you know where Scott Jacobs is now?"

"No, after the accident, he felt so bad he just quit. I haven't heard from him since."

"One last question, you wouldn't happen to have Hiram Webster's telephone number would you?"

"Oh, Hiram is dead, but his wife Nancy is still alive. I can give you her number. She moved you know."

"Mr. Webster is dead? When did he die?"

"About a month or two ago. Poor man had a heart attack."

"I see. Yes, could I have Nancy Webster's number please?"

After getting Mrs. Webster's telephone number, I thanked Mrs. Markley for her time and hung up. I made a few notes and took a few minutes to digest the conversations. By the time I'd finished, Sandra and Jackson had arrived and were helping Lilly get dinner on the table.

I locked everything up in my safe and joined them in the kitchen.

I really wasn't in the mood for company, but managed to hold up my end of the conversation during dinner.

Jackson received a phone call from the police department just as he finished eating and left.

After dinner I fed the dogs while Lilly and Sandra were cleaning the kitchen.

"Lilly, where's Max? I haven't seen that cat all day?" I asked.

"Oh, I'm not sure dear. I fed him while you were on the phone. I'm sure he's around here somewhere," Lilly answered absently.

I wandered through the house looking for Max and finally found him curled up on my bed.

I'd never owned a cat before, and found myself becoming quite attached. I settled on the bed next to him and started to pet him. He stretched, yawned, and then settled back down next to me and began to emit an awesome purr.

I wrapped my arm around him and drew him close, then felt myself begin to drift off to sleep.

Chapter Twelve

I awoke with a start, still in my clothes and with Max curled up beside me. Someone had covered me with a blanket at one point during the night.

I allowed myself a few minutes of cuddling with Max before getting out of bed and heading for the shower.

As I was getting dressed, I heard the rattle of pots and pans from the kitchen and Lilly talking to the dogs while preparing breakfast.

I felt a little guilty. I hadn't really spent any time with Lilly or the dogs lately, but this case really had me going. I felt like I was chasing my tail.

"Good morning, Dear! Did you sleep well?" Lilly asked brightly as I joined her in the kitchen and poured myself a cup of coffee.

"Like a rock," I answered with a chuckle as I poured myself a cup of coffee.

"Well, you needed it. You've been working way too hard lately," she said, deftly flipping a pancake.

"I know. But I have to figure this out."

"What's the main point of contention, other than who killed Madame Phoebe?"

"The skull. There has to be something about that skull. I just wish I knew more about it. Maybe tonight I'll have time to research crystal skulls a little bit. I have other things to take care of today," I answered wistfully.

"Anything I can help you with?" she asked.

"Do you know how to use the Internet?"

"No, is it difficult?"

"Not really once you get the hang of it. I'll show you later."

"Great!"

I finished breakfast and retrieved my notes from the safe in my den.

"Lilly?" I said, walking into the kitchen.

Lilly jumped in fright and dropped a crystal glass on the floor that she'd been rinsing out. The glass shattered into a million pieces.

"Lilly! I'm sorry. Watch the glass!"

"Oh, Savannah! I'm so sorry. You scared me."

"It's okay," I said, staring at the glass on the floor.

Lilly bent down to start picking up the shards of glass from the floor.

"No! Don't touch it!"

"Why not?"

Without answering her, I slowly circled the pieces of glass on the floor.

"Lilly, is there a heavy crystal glass in the cabinet?" I asked, never taking my eyes off the broken glass on the floor.

"Yes, a big thick one. Why?"

"Hand it to me please," I said, extending my hand.

Lilly handed me a heavy glass from the cabinet.

I took the glass and dropped it on the hardwood floor of the kitchen. It didn't break.

"Lilly, do me a favor. Today I need you to go out and find something made out of crystal that's about the same size as the skull," I said, picking the glass off the floor.

"Okay. But why?"

"I'll explain later. I have to go," I said, grabbing my bag off the counter.

"Bye Dear. Have a good day," she said reaching for the broom and dustpan to clean up the mess.

I got to the office and started a pot of coffee. After making sure I had my notes in front of me, I dialed Nancy Webster's number.

"Hello?" A soft voice said into the phone.

"Hello. Is this Nancy Webster?" I asked politely.

"Yes it is," she said tentatively.

"Mrs. Webster, my name's Savannah Williams and I'm a private detective. I got your number from Rebecca Markley. Do you have a minute?"

"Yes of course. What could I possibly help you with Ms. Williams?"

I'm calling about the crystal skull that Arthur Friedman purchased from you."

"Oh that dreadful skull. How is Arthur?"

"Oh, Mrs. Webster, I thought you knew."

"Knew what, Ms. Williams?" she asked in confusion.

"I'm sorry to have to be the one to tell you this, Mrs. Webster, but Arthur Friedman is dead," I said solemnly.

"Dead! When! How?"

"Arthur Friedman died in a car accident about two weeks ago."

"Oh my dear that's terrible," she said sadly.

"Yes it is," I agreed.

"I'm sorry, Ms. Williams, it's just that Arthur and I have known each other for years."

"I understand. Now about the skull," I said, trying to turn the conversation back in the right direction.

"Oh, yes, the skull. What did you want to know?"

"What can you tell me about it?"

"Oh, that skull has been the brunt of jokes among all of us since Rubin found it in Mexico. Rubin loved that thing so. Then he gave it to Thomas Markley and then my husband Hiram had it. When Hiram died, I sold it to Arthur for the museum."

"Yes, I know that much, what I really want to know is what is so special about that skull?"

"I really don't know. But I can tell you this. Thomas Markley told his wife never to sell the skull, that it was worth a fortune."

"Well, then why did Mrs. Markley sell it to Hiram?"

"Oh, she hated that skull. She said it gave her the creeps. Besides, she took it to a jeweler to be appraised. The jeweler told her because it had been broken and put back together its worth greatly diminished."

"Okay, then why did Arthur Friedman pay two hundred thousand dollars for it?"

"That's what he offered me for it. I told him that it had only been appraised at eighty thousand or so, but he said that he would pay his original offer of two hundred thousand dollars. Personally, I think it was his way of making sure I was taken care of. You see, while my husband was successful, we weren't well off. I think it was Arthur's way of insuring my financial security," she explained.

"I see," I said tentatively, not quite convinced.

"Arthur made up that Certificate of Authenticity for me to sign so that he would have the proper paperwork to display the skull at the museum."

"But, the Certificate of Authenticity really isn't doing that Mrs. Webster. All it says is that you swear it was the same skull found by Rubin Fleming in the Mayan ruins in Mexico. There is no way to know for sure if it is the same skull, although I'm convinced it is."

"I see your point, Ms. Williams, but that's all I know."

"Yes, I'm sure it is. Well, thank you for your time Mrs. Webster."

"Oh, you're more than welcome Ms. Williams, please, call again if I can be of any further help."

"Oh, I will. Thank you. Good-bye."

Deciding to follow through on a theory that had been eating away at me all morning, I dialed Mrs. Markley's phone number.

"Hello?" Mrs. Markley said after the third ring.

"Hello, Mrs. Markley, this is Savannah Williams."

"Oh, hello, Ms. Williams."

"Listen, I just have one quick question if it's okay."

"Of course. What did you need?"

"What was the floor of Thomas' shop made of?"

"Well, the front part of the shop where the customers were waited on was carpeted. Behind the counters there was beautiful tile on the floor."

"Great. Was there a back room to the store?"

"Yes, Thomas' office, several repair stations, and a small storage room."

"What was on the floor in those rooms?"

"They were cement."

"Where did Mr. Markley keep the skull?"

"On a shelf in his office."

"Okay, about how high off the ground was the shelf?"

"Oh, five or six feet I would suppose," she answered after pausing to think for a moment.

"Great. Thanks Mrs. Markley, you've been a great help," I said.

"Your welcome, Ms. Williams. Keep in touch now."

"I will," I promised and hung up the phone.

I spent a few minutes making notes, then got up and began to pace the office. My theory clicked into place, now I just had to prove it.

Feeling restless, I donned my coat and gloves and decided to take a walk through town to clear my head.

After stopping at the drug store for a large hot chocolate, I strolled through town to the park by the lake.

I must have been deep in thought, because I didn't even hear Jackson approach.

"Hey, Savannah," Jackson said, sitting down next to me on the bench.

"Jackson! You scared me half to death," I exclaimed, jumping in fright.

"Sorry," he said hiding a smile.

"It's okay. What are you doing out here?"

"I saw you walking to the park from my office window and decided to join you," he said, putting his arm around me and pulling me close.

"I'm glad you did," I said, snuggling up to him.

"Listen, why would my Mom call and ask me if I knew someone that knew a lot about computers?" he asked.

"Oh, I asked her if she knew how to use the Internet."

"Oh, because I sent Detective Marshall, our resident computer genius, over there," he said.

"You did what!" I exclaimed, almost jumping to my feet.

"Problem?"

"Oh my God. I have to go," I said, leaping off the bench.

"What did I do?" Jackson asked, scurrying to keep up with my blistering pace down the sidewalk toward my office.

"I think you created a monster," I said breathlessly as we reached my office.

I raced up the stairs to my office and grabbed my bag and the box with the crystal skull in it out of my safe then headed home.

"Lilly!" I yelled walking into the house and depositing my bag and the box on the counter.

"We're upstairs Dear!" Lilly called down from her sitting room.

I took the stairs two at a time up to Lilly's sitting room. Lilly and Detective Marshall were huddled together at the roll top desk.

"Savannah, I bought a computer and printer this morning," Lilly said proudly, moving aside to reveal a laptop computer on her desk.

"That's great," I said warily.

"Yes, and Detective Marshall put in a wireless network so I can get online from up here! Isn't that great!" she said, her cheeks flushed with excitement.

"He did what!"

"A wireless network. Very efficient," Detective Marshall said.

"I see," I said, none to pleased that I wasn't consulted.

"Well, I've got to get back to the station, Lilly, call me if you have any questions," Detective Marshall said, rising from his chair.

"Okay, thank you for helping me with this," Lilly said, her eyes never leaving the screen.

"My pleasure. Bye," Detective Marshall said, bounding out of the room and down the stairs.

"Savannah, now I can research the crystal skulls on the Internet for you," Lilly said.

"The crystal skulls," I said.

"Yes, isn't that wonderful?."

"Wonderful. Did you manage to get something about the size of the skull while you were out buying your computer?" I asked.

"Oh yes. It's perfect. It's a crystal sculpture. I put it on your desk," she said absently, her attention riveted to the computer screen.

"Thanks," I said and trudged back down the stairs to my office.

Sitting on my desk was a crystal statue of a woman. I lifted it up and found it to be about the same size and density as the crystal skull. I took the statue and headed down the basement stairs to perform a small experiment.

I stood on a small stepladder, held the statue above my head and let it fall to the concrete floor of the basement.

The statue broke into five or six large pieces on impact. A few small shards of glass skidded across the basement floor.

"Just as I thought," I said out loud studying the broken statue. "The skull wasn't dropped, it was taken apart."

Chapter Thirteen

Filled with sudden inspiration, I raced up the basement stairs and grabbed my bag and the box with the skull in it off the counter in the kitchen.

"I'll be back later, Lilly! Sorry about the mess in the basement!" I hollered up the stairs.

"Okay! Dinner's at six!"

I drove into town and parked in front of Brody's Jewelers. I grabbed the box off the passenger seat and walked into the jewelry store.

An older man stood behind one of the counters waiting on a customer. The man appeared to be in his late sixties and short and stocky in stature. His gray hair had receded, but was combed neatly. His bright blue eyes were clear and friendly.

"I'll be right with you, Miss," he said cheerfully.

"Okay. Thank you," I said browsing the display cases. I wanted to buy Lilly something for being so special and taking such good care of the dogs, Max and me.

I was just starting to look at the gold necklaces when the customer left the store.

"May I help you with something?" The older man asked.

"Yes, a couple of things actually."

"My pleasure. I'm Sylvester Brody."

"Savannah Williams."

"Now, what may I help you with?"

"I'm looking for a gift for an older woman. Something special, but not too fancy."

"Did you have something in mind?"

"Maybe a necklace, but something plain, she's not a real flashy woman."

After several minutes of looking, I finally decided on a herringbone pattern gold chain.

"Excellent choice," Mr. Brody said in approval as he carefully placed the necklace in a black velvet box.

"Thank you," I said smiling, tucking the jewelry box into my bag.

"Now, why don't you tell me the real reason for your visit," he said astutely.

"Okay. You caught me," I laughed.

I carefully unpacked the crystal skull from the box and set it on the top of one of the display cases.

"I need you to open this skull."

"Open it! What on earth for?" he asked in amazement as he examined the skull with awe.

"Well, if you look at it closely, you'll notice a hairline crease running up the center of the skull and a small hole on the bottom. The skull has already been taken apart and put back together at some point in time. I want to know why."

Mr. Brody picked up the skull and looked at it closely.

"My eyes just aren't what they used to be I'm afraid. Would you mind if I took this in the back and looked at it under a magnifying lamp?" he said sheepishly.

"Be my guest."

"I'll be just a minute," he said, excusing himself.

I waited patiently while Mr. Brody examined the skull. Watching him through the door opening I could tell he was very meticulous in his examination. After a few minutes he returned with the skull.

"Amazing," he said somewhat confused.

"What's amazing?"

"I can't understand why someone would take apart such an ancient relic," he said shaking his head.

"That's what I want you to find out. Can you take the skull apart?"

"Well, yes. The skull was put back together with jeweler's epoxy. It shouldn't be too difficult to use epoxy solvent and get it apart."

"Is it something I could do myself?"

"Well, not without some difficulty. You see epoxy solvent can be quite tricky to use sometimes. But I would be more than happy to let you watch while I take it apart, although it's going to take quite a long time."

"That would be great. Is there any other way to get the skull apart without damaging the crystal?"

"Well, I suppose I could saw it in half. That's how it was opened in the first place."

"It was sawed in half?"

"Yes, with a diamond bladed saw. It's the only thing that will go through crystal this thick," he explained.

"Saw away then," I said with a slight grimace.

"Don't worry, Ms. Williams, the skull won't be damaged," he smiled.

"Okay. Can I watch?"

"Of course. Follow me," he said gallantly.

I followed Mr. Brody into the back room of the store filled with all types of machinery and tools for very delicate work.

He approached a small saw anchored on one of the workbenches. I watched as he carefully adjusted the saw to the right depth and angle. A few minutes later he started up the saw and put the skull into place.

I couldn't bear to watch as the saw blade began to cut through the skull.

Within a few minutes, he flipped off the saw and carefully carried the skull over to another workbench that had a thick, black velvet pad on it. He laid the skull down and picked up a small, delicate hammer and gave the skull a gentle tap.

The skull separated into two pieces revealing a hollowed out area in the base of the skull just behind the mouth area. Inside this space lay a white drawstring pouch.

"Well, what have we got here?" he asked.

"Let's find out," I said, picking up the pouch.

I opened the drawstring and dumped the contents of the pouch into my hand.

A huge thick crystal appearing stone fell into the palm of my hand.

We both gasped in awe as the light caught the stone causing it to sparkle brilliantly.

"What is it?" I asked, my voice barely above a whisper.

"Let's see," he said, picking up a jeweler's glass off the workbench.

I handed the stone to Mr. Brody who spent quite a few minutes examining every inch of it.

"It's a diamond. The best I've ever seen. It's flawless," he said, his eyes wide with wonder.

"Unbelievable," I whispered, staring at the diamond.

"If this diamond is what I think it is, its much more than that, Ms. Williams," he said, handing the diamond back to me.

"What do you think it is?" I asked with baited breath.

"Well, I can't be sure without doing some research, but, have you ever heard of the Star of Angels diamond?" he asked.

"Yes, but I don't know much about it," I admitted.

"Well, the Star of Angels diamond was found in the mid-nineteen hundreds in a mine in South Africa. It's the biggest diamond ever discovered. When it was discovered, there was a smooth cleavage on one side of the diamond leading people to believe that it had once been part of a larger diamond. As you can imagine, rumors began to spread about the diamond. Even rumors that the miner who found the diamond, had found both halves of the diamond and kept the other half for himself. Soon after the Star of Angels was discovered, the miner quit the mine and moved back to the United States. It's my belief that this might be that diamond. It's got to be over six hundred carats," he explained.

"What makes you think this is the missing half of the Star of Angels diamond?"

"Much has been written about the Star of Angels, Ms. Williams. I've been fascinated with that diamond for years, and have studied it extensively. There are certain shared characteristics between this diamond and the Star of Angels diamond."

"Wow, so this diamond is worth a small fortune," I surmised.

"More like a very large fortune," he said seriously.

"Well that certainly explains a lot," I said, picking up the diamond and placing it carefully back into the drawstring pouch.

"I'm sorry?" he asked in confusion.

"It explains why everybody wants to get their hands on this skull," I said thoughtfully.

"I understand."

"Mr. Brody, do you know the name of that miner who is believed to have stolen the other half of the Star of Angels diamond?"

"Not off the top of my head. But I can look it up for you tonight when I get home."

"That would be wonderful. Here's my card."

I jotted my home telephone number on the back of the card and handed it to Mr. Brody.

"Oh, you're a private detective," he said with interest.

"Yes."

"What do you plan on doing with the diamond, if I may ask?" he said.

"I'm going fishing, Mr. Brody, and this is the bait," I answered mysteriously tucking the pouch into a zippered compartment of my bag.

"Ahhhh."

"Could you please glue the skull back together for me?"

"Of course," he said, turning his attention to the skull.

"Mr. Brody. I'm afraid I have inadvertently put you in a very bad position. I can't even begin to tell you how important it is that you not tell anyone about this," I cautioned.

"I understand. If anybody asks, I will simply say that you came in to buy a gift," he said, as he worked on the skull.

"Great, but I'm afraid that someone might have seen me carry this box into the store. I've been followed recently," I explained.

"Then I shall simply tell anyone who asks specifically about the skull, that that I performed an appraisal for you," he said calmly.

111

"Okay. But if anyone asks about the skull, could you telephone me immediately with a description of the person?"

"With pleasure. I should tell you that I'll be out of town for the next couple of weeks. I'm taking my wife on a well-deserved vacation, so the store will be closed after today. My son will be stopping by daily to check on things for me."

"That's even better," I said with relief.

"There. Good as new. Leave the tape on for the next twenty-four hours until the epoxy fully sets up," he said, examining his handy work with a critical eye.

"Thank you, Mr. Brody. How much do I owe you?" I said, carefully repacking the skull in its box.

After paying him, I carried the skull back to my Jeep and drove the short block to my office, locking the skull in my safe.

I spent quite a bit of time answering my e-mail and returning phone calls. Before I knew it, it was almost six o'clock.

Lilly would kill me if I was late for dinner. I hastily put away all my paperwork and, after setting the alarm, locked the office and drove home.

"You're late," Lilly greeted me as I flew through the door of the house.

"Sorry. I got caught up in paperwork," I said meekly, as heading into my den.

After locking the diamond in the safe, I rushed back into the kitchen and took my place at the table, tucking the jewelry box with Lilly's necklace in it up the sleeve of my sweater.

"Hi, Jackson," I said, realizing he was sitting at the table with an amused smile playing around his mouth.

"Busy day?" he asked as he poured me a glass of wine.

"Very," I said, taking a long sip.

I slyly placed the velvet jewelry box on Lilly's plate while she scooped the steamed asparagus onto a serving plate at the stove.

"What's this?" Lilly asked, as she came to the table.

"Just a little something to say that I really appreciate having you here," I smiled.

"Oh, Savannah! It's beautiful!" she said, after opening the box.

"I hoped you'd like it," I answered with relief. I'm horrible at picking out presents.

"Oh thank you, Dear!" she said, giving me a hug.

"You're welcome, Lilly."

"Jackson, put this on for me," she said, holding out the necklace.

Jackson rose and took the necklace from Lilly. After fastening the clasp on the necklace he returned to his chair.

"How does it look?" she asked, her face wreathed in smiles.

"It looks beautiful."

"I have to go look," she said, leaving the table and going into the half bath to look at herself in the mirror.

"Oh, it's perfect," she gushed returning to the table.

"Just like you, Mom," Jackson said sweetly, squeezing Lilly's hand.

"Oh, Jackson. You tease so," Lilly said, blushing deeply.

After dinner, Jackson and I settled in on the couch to watch a movie. Lilly retreated to her sitting room upstairs to play on the Internet.

Midway into the movie I fell asleep as usual. Jackson woke me up when the movie was over, and after letting him out the front door, I set the alarm and went to bed.

Chapter Fourteen

I felt someone gently shake my shoulder early the next morning. I rolled over and opened my eyes to find Lilly perched over my bed.

"Sorry to wake you, but you have a telephone call. The man said it's important," she said.

"Thanks, Lilly," I answered, still not fully awake.

I clamored over the dogs and Max to reach the cordless telephone on the nightstand next to my bed.

"Hello," I yawned into the telephone.

"Sorry to call so early, Ms. Williams. This is Sylvester Brody from the jewelry store."

"Oh, Mr. Brody. What can I do for you?" I asked, sitting up in bed.

"I found the name of that miner for you."

"Great. What is it?"

"His name was Thomas Markley."

I inhaled sharply at the news.

"Are you sure?"

"Positive. Also, I went back through the information on the Star of Angels diamond, and the characteristics of the diamond you have and the Star of Angels diamond are identical," he exclaimed.

"So, you're telling me that I have the missing half of the Star of Angels diamond?" I said, barely breathing.

"Exactly," he confirmed.

"Wow. So who does the diamond really belong to then?" I said, my mind racing at break neck speed. This whole case just got a lot more complicated.

"Technically, it would belong to the owner of the mine I suppose. But that mine has been shut down for years. I guess it would be up to the courts to decide," he said.

"I suppose. Do you happen to know who owned the mine?"

"A company called Nazareth Diamond Mines," he answered.

"Thanks."

"What do you plan on doing with the diamond?" he asked.

"I guess after this case is resolved, I'll turn it over to the authorities and let them deal with it from there," I answered honestly.

"That would be for the best I'm sure. Good luck, Ms. Williams."

"Thanks. Enjoy your vacation."

"Thank you. Good-bye."

"Bye," I said, absently hanging up the telephone.

I crawled out of bed and after donning my robe headed out into the kitchen for breakfast.

"What's this?" I asked picking up some papers from my place at the table.

"I did some research on the crystal skulls last night. I thought it might help," Lilly answered as she poured me a cup of coffee.

"Thanks," I said and settled in at the table.

I spent breakfast reading over the information Lilly had gathered on crystal skulls.

There seemed to be discrepancies between the so-called experts as to how many ancient skulls were actually known and their theories varied as to what they were used for.

One theory is that the skulls were brought down by aliens and given to the ancient people. Another theory said that when all the skulls were put together, they would start to talk or sing and reveal information important to the survival of mankind.

There also appeared to be much debate on how the skulls were carved and created.

The material the skulls were made of varied also. While some were made out of crystal of varying degrees of clarity, some were made out of clear to cloudy quartz. There was even a skull that made of rose quartz with a removable jaw.

I finished breakfast and filed the papers in my safe along with the rest of the case files. I'd just closed the safe when the telephone rang.

"Savannah! It's for you!" Lilly hollered in from the kitchen.

"Okay! Thanks!" I replied and clamored down the spiral staircase to the phone.

"Savannah Williams," I said breathlessly into the phone.

"Hey darlin, its Clint."

"Hey, Clint. What's up?"

"I did some more digging on that DePaulo you asked me about. I'm not sure if this will help, but I found out a little more information."

"Really?"

"Yes. Seems Viktor DePaulo's real name is Viktor Nazareth. As Viktor Nazareth he has no record, so that would explain why his fingerprints were put in the system as belonging to Viktor DePaulo."

"Nazareth. Interesting. Listen, can you run a company called Nazareth Diamond Mines through your magic computer and tell me who owned it?"

"Sure thing. Hang on a sec," he said. I heard him punch a few keys on his keyboard.

"Whoa!"

"What?" I asked.

"Good hunch. The registered agent to the mine is Viktor Nazareth. The mine shut down about ten years ago."

"Wow! No wonder DePaulo is so anxious to get his hands on the skull. Can you fax me that?"

"No problem. It's on the way. I have to go. Be careful, Savannah," he cautioned.

"I will, and thanks, Clint."

Seconds later the fax machine whirled into action and I spent a few minutes making some notes then locking the papers in my safe. It's definitely going to be a busy day.

Chapter Fifteen

It seemed like it took me forever to get dressed. I had a hard time finding a shirt baggy enough to hide the bulge of the gun holster threaded through my belt. I finally decided on a baggy navy blue sweatshirt and a pair of jeans. I retrieved the diamond from my safe and headed into Mt. Clements for my first stop of the day.

Arriving at the Museum of Ancient History at precisely nine o'clock, I gave my name to the receptionist and requested to see Paul Friedman.

Within a minute or two I saw Paul coming down the short hallway in my direction.

"Savannah. To what do I owe the pleasure?" he asked with a hint of sarcasm in his voice.

"I need to talk to you in private."

"As you wish. Coffee?" he asked.

"No thank you."

I followed Paul into his office and once we were settled, reached into my bag for the diamond.

"I have something to show you," I said, carefully opening the drawstrings on the pouch.

"Oh?"

"Now, why don't you tell me the whole story about the crystal skull, Paul?" I said, casually laying the diamond on his desk.

I watched his eyes widen in awe of the beautiful diamond, and then watched as his expression turned from awe to fear.

"How did you find the diamond?" he asked, his eyes never leaving the glistening gem, his voice barely above a whisper.

"I'm a detective remember? It's my job."

"Point taken. Yes, I knew about the diamond," he said with a note of resignation in his voice.

"Tell me how."

"My father was actually the one who told me about it. You see Thomas Markley and my father were in the Army together. They were stationed in South America. After their terms were up, my father returned to the States. Thomas Markley stayed in South America and got a job in a diamond mine. When he got back from South America, he took over his father's jewelry store. My father and him stayed in touch through the years and our families vacationed together frequently. I assume it was during one of these vacations that my father found out about the diamond."

"That would make sense. But, what was your father planning to do with the diamond once he acquired it? Technically, its stolen property."

"That I honestly don't know. I asked him about that and he chose not to answer me. He just told me not to worry about it, that it was his affair, not mine," he answered bitterly.

"So why not just tell me about the diamond the first time we met?"

"Because I didn't want you to think I'd killed Madame Phoebe to get the diamond."

"I see. Well, despite what you have told me, you are still a suspect." I said, picking up the diamond and replacing it in the pouch.

"Why? I've told you what I know!"

"Because you had motive and opportunity. Have a nice day, Mr. Friedman," I said, placing the pouch in my bag and walking out of his office.

"One down and two to go," I said out loud backing out of my parking space.

I dialed Amy Conterri's cell phone number as I turned onto Main Street.

"Hello," Amy answered.

"Hi Amy, it's Savannah Williams. Can you meet me somewhere? I need to talk to you."

"I'm at Phoebe's store cleaning and packing so the landlord can rent the space. Do you want to meet me here?"

"Perfect. I'm two minutes away. See you soon," I said.

The second I hung up my phone, it rang.

"Savannah Williams."

"Hi Savannah, it's Detective Wilder."

"Hi Detective. What's up?" I asked, pulling into a parking space in front of Madame Phoebe's store.

"Arthur Friedman was murdered," he confirmed.

"I thought so."

"Forensics found that the brake line of his car had a small slice in it. Once the brake fluid all drained out, there would be no way he could stop the car. Given the icy road conditions the night he died, he didn't stand a chance."

"I see. So, do you think there's a chance that it was just meant as a warning or do you think murder was the intention all along?"

"Hard to say. It could be either way."

"True. Oh, I know why everyone wants the skull."

"Really? Why?"

"I don't want to say over the phone. I'm at Madame Phoebe's store to meet with Amy. I'll stop by your office in about twenty minutes if that's okay?"

"Sure thing. See you then."

"Okay. Later," I said and hung up the phone.

I let myself into Madame Phoebe's store with the key Detective Wilder had given me.

Amy stood in the back room boxing up some odds and ends.

"Hi, Amy."

"Oh, hi, Savannah," she said, taping up a box.

"What are you going to do with all this stuff?" I asked, looking around.

"I'm not sure yet. I'm hoping I can return most of it to the distributors. I know you and Phoebe were friends. If there's something you see that you want, please take it," she said surveying the small mountain of boxes stacked against one of the walls.

"Thank you. I'll look around on my way out."

"Listen Amy, I found out why Phoebe was killed."

"Really? It's that skull isn't it?"

"Not exactly. It's what was in the skull."

I withdrew the pouch from my bag, pulled out the diamond and placed it in the palm of my hand.

"Wow," she said, her eyes growing wide at the sight of the diamond.

"Quite a motive for murder isn't it?" I asked, my gaze never leaving her face.

"It must be worth a small fortune," she whispered.

"I imagine it is," I answered replacing the diamond in the pouch and putting it back into my bag.

"Did Phoebe know about the diamond?"

"I don't know. I was hoping you could tell me."

"I honestly don't think she did. I think that she thought the skull was special because of her beliefs in the paranormal."

"Probably."

"So what are you going to do with it?"

"Turn it over to the authorities when the case is settled. Anyway, I have to go."

"Listen, before you go, could you watch the store for a second, I want to run down the street to the deli and grab a sandwich and something to drink. It's just such a pain to have to lock up the store. I'll be right back."

"Sure. Go ahead."

"Thanks," she said grabbing her purse.

I watched her walk out of the store and locked the door behind her taking the opportunity to browse through the opened boxes in the main part of the store. Madame Phoebe had a wide variety of crystals and I remembered seeing one that would be very useful right about now.

After a brief search, I found a crystal about the same size, shape and color as the diamond that I quickly tucked into my bag. A couple of minutes later, Amy returned with a sandwich and drink.

"Okay. Thanks. Keep in touch won't you?" she asked.

"Yes, I will. Oh, by the way, could I have the key to Madame Phoebe's townhouse for a couple of days? I want to take another look around."

"Oh, sure."

She retrieved a set of keys out of her purse and after extracting a key from the key ring, handed it to me.

"Thanks," I said, tucking the key in the pocket of my jeans.

"Talk to you later?"

"Yes, I'll call you in a couple of days. Bye."

"Bye."

I walked out of the store and locked the door behind me. Walking back to my Jeep, I saw DePaulo's men in the black Grand Am parked across the street from Madame Phoebe's store. I walked over to the car. One of the men rolled down the driver's side window.

"Give a message to your boss for me."

"What's that?" The man asked gruffly.

"Tell DePaulo that I need to meet with him. Tell him to meet me at my office at two. Tell him to come alone," I said, and without waiting for a reply, walked to my truck.

Out of my rear view mirror I saw the driver make a call on his cell phone. Good. Message delivered.

I drove to the Mt. Clements police station and quickly filled Detective Wilder in on what I'd learned.

"Wow, that's some story." he said.

"Yes, it is."

"So, who all knew about the diamond then?"

"As far as I can gather, Arthur Friedman, Paul Friedman, Thomas Markley, DePaulo, and maybe Madame Phoebe," I answered.

"So you don't think Amy Conterri knew about the diamond?"

"I don't know," I answered honestly.

"What makes you think Phoebe knew?"

"Because of the note she put in the box with the skull. In her note, she said that I was the only one she could trust to keep the skull safe and that she would explain when I went to see her at her shop. Unfortunately she was murdered before I even got the skull."

"Okay, that makes sense. So based on what you've told me, and the fact that Arthur Friedman was murdered, Paul Friedman and DePaulo have just moved to the top of the suspect list."

"I would say so. Yes."

"Now about the diamond, where is it?"

"In a safety deposit box."

If Detective Wilder knew what I was up to, he would never allow it.

"You are planning on turning it over as evidence aren't you?" he asked.

"Oh yes of course. I just didn't want to run all over town carrying it."

"I agree. In fact, I'm not sure I want something that valuable in the evidence locker here either. It's probably as safe as it can get right where it is."

"I agree. Why don't I just keep it there, and when this whole mess is settled, we'll turn it over to the proper authorities," I suggested.

"That's probably best."

"Okay. I'll keep in touch. I have to go," I said, anxious to make a hasty retreat.

"Okay. See you later," he said rising from his chair.

Detective Wilder walked me out to my Jeep and we said good-bye. I saw no sign of the DePaulo's men in the black Grand Am as I pulled out of the police station. They'd probably gone to pick up their boss for our meeting.

On my way to my office, I drove through Taco Bell to get some lunch. After opening my office, I took a much-needed break to eat and make some notes. I'd already decided I wasn't going to reveal to DePaulo that I knew his connection to the diamond mine. A girl has got to have some secrets.

I placed the pouch with the diamond in it in the center of my desk. At precisely two o'clock, DePaulo walked through the door of my office.

"Mr. DePaulo, how nice to see you again," I said, rising to greet him.

"The pleasure is all mine, I assure you," he said gallantly, kissing my hand.

"Please come in. Would you care for some coffee, or perhaps a cold beverage?" I asked.

"No, thank you. My associates said that you needed to speak with me?" he said, settling comfortably into one of the chairs across from my desk.

"Yes. Thank you for coming alone," I answered, taking my place behind my desk.

"You have reconsidered my offer for the crystal skull then?"

"Yes, in a matter of speaking. If your client still wishes to purchase the skull, I'm sure that can be arranged. However, I don't think your client will still be interested in the skull since it's missing its contents," I said, choosing my words carefully, putting sarcastic emphasis on the word 'client'

"I'm sorry. I don't follow," he said, furrowing his brow.

"The diamond hidden inside the skull, Mr. DePaulo, that's what your client is really interested in isn't it?" I asked.

"Diamond? I'm afraid you have me at a disadvantage, Ms. Williams. I know of no diamond."

"Oh come now, Mr. DePaulo, you can't expect me to believe that you know nothing of this?"

I said, carefully taking the diamond out of its pouch and setting it on my desk.

"How did you ever find that?" he said in a strangled voice.

"It's my job," I answered, picking up the diamond and replacing it in its pouch.

"I see that we have much to talk about, Ms. Williams," he said, regaining his composure.

"Yes, I think we do. You first."

"To tell you the truth, Ms. Williams, I'd heard rumors about the missing half of the Star of Angels diamond, but I wasn't even sure the diamond really existed."

"So, you were following a hunch?"

"Yes, so to speak."

"That still doesn't explain why Arthur Friedman was so afraid of you knowing he had the skull," I said.

"I can assure you, Ms. Williams, Arthur Friedman had no reason to fear me. I am, as I told you, not prone to violence. I'm sure we could have worked out a mutually agreeable settlement. However, Arthur Friedman was tragically killed in an automobile accident before we could meet."

"Then how did you track the skull to Madame Phoebe, and then to me? Oh, never mind, I can answer that."

"Yes?" he prodded.

"You followed the same path I did tracking the skull's whereabouts. You tried to set up a meeting with Arthur Friedman, but he wouldn't meet with you. Then your associates tried to scare him into meeting with you by rigging the brakes on his car to fail. But that backfired because Arthur Friedman was killed. Having no other choice, your associates broke into the Museum of Ancient History looking for the skull after Arthur

Friedman's death. They didn't find the skull, but found a copy of the letter Arthur Friedman sent to Madame Phoebe. From there, you and your associates went to Madame Phoebe's store to get the skull by whatever means necessary. Madame Phoebe wouldn't tell you where she hid the skull, so you killed her and ransacked the store. You couldn't find the skull, but you did find my card on a bulletin board above Madame Phoebe's desk and that's how your search led to me. But you weren't sure I had the skull until your associates saw me with it through the window to my den. Is that about how it went Mr. DePaulo?" I asked, my eyes flashing in anger.

"I can assure you, Ms. Williams, neither myself nor my associates had anything to do with the death of Arthur Friedman, or Madame Phoebe. As for the rest of your theory, it makes for interesting fiction. I must go. I have another meeting to attend. I will be in touch," he said evenly, rising from his chair.

"Count on it," I said, returning his gaze.

Without another word, DePaulo left my office. I watched out the windows of my office as he climbed into the backseat of his black Lincoln. The Lincoln roared to life and I heard the screeching of tires as it rapidly drove out of sight.

I took the diamond out of its pouch, and replaced it with the crystal from Madame Phoebe's store. After wrapping it in a few layers of paper towel, I placed it in a manila envelope. After depositing the diamond in my safety deposit box, I walked back to my office to make some notes on the conversation with DePaulo.

I'd rattled a lot of people's cages today. It would be interesting to see who would rattle mine back.

Chapter Sixteen

Sometimes in the middle of a case the thing a private detective fears most happens. There's no way to stop it, no way to explain it; it just happens; the case comes to a screeching halt.

When this annoying phenomenon rears its ugly head there's only one thing to do, start at the beginning.

That's the situation I found myself in leaving my office around three thirty. About the only thing I could do was wait for the killer to make his or her move; a totally unacceptable option.

After stopping at the office supply store I headed home. Lilly was gone, so I grabbed a cookie off the plate on the counter and headed into my den.

I'd purchased a large display board at the store and set it up on the floor of my den. In order to start at the beginning, I had to fully understand where I'd been. After retrieving my case notes from the safe, I got down to business.

I divided the display board into three sections, means, motive, and opportunity.

I took an index card and printed Paul Friedman's name on it in big black letters and secured it to the board with a red pushpin.

Paul Friedman certainly had the means to murder both Madame Phoebe and his father. It was obvious that Paul's relationship with his father was less than ideal.

As for Paul murdering Madame Phoebe, there were still doubts. He denied knowing Madame Phoebe personally, but he could be lying. No, Paul Friedman, certainly had the means to commit both murders.

The motive was simple. He was after the diamond in the skull. Opportunity was also easy. It would be a piece of cake for him to cut the brake line on his father's car, and no one at the museum can really account for his whereabouts during the time of Madame Phoebe's murder. The Museum lays only three blocks away from Madame Phoebe's store. Paul had ample opportunity to murder Madame Phoebe and be back at the museum before even being missed.

I wrote all the information on index cards and tacked them to the display board under the appropriate heading. As I placed the last index card under Paul Friedman's name, a question occurred to me.

I dialed Detective Wilder's cell phone number.

"Detective Wilder," he answered on the second ring.

"Hi, Detective. It's Savannah. I have a question."

"Oh, hi, Savannah. Hopefully I have an answer," he said laughing.

"Does Arthur Friedman's widow know her husband was murdered?"

"She does now, so does Paul. I just left their house."

"Oh? How'd they take the news?"

"Mrs. Friedman was shocked. She couldn't imagine why anyone would want to kill her husband. Paul Friedman was angry."

"Angry?"

"Yes. He threw a good old-fashioned temper tantrum. Started pacing the room and ranting and raving."

"What did he say?"

"He said that he couldn't believe his father was murdered, who would want to do such a thing, you know the routine."

"That's interesting. When I first met with Paul Friedman he alluded vaguely to the fact that his father had been murdered. It should have come to no real surprise to him," I mused, making a few notes.

"Maybe he just put on an act for the benefit of his mother." he suggested.

"Could be."

"Just another piece of the puzzle."

"Sure is. I think I'll wait a day or so, but I'm going to make a call on Paul's mother. What is her first name?"

"Virginia. Virginia Friedman, but she prefers to be called Ginny," he answered.

"Okay. Thanks. I'll talk to you later."

"Sure thing. Keep in touch."

I made a few notes then turned my attention back to the task at hand moving on to my second suspect, Viktor DePaulo, a/k/a Viktor Nazareth.

There was no question in my mind that DePaulo and his two henchmen were involved in this case up to their big, bushy eyebrows. But whether they'd committed the murders was still up for debate. DePaulo had good reason for wanting to get his hands on that skull, and as much as I hated to admit it, I was pretty sure the diamond legally belonged to him because he'd owned the mine.

I made a note to find out the names of his two henchmen. I knew nothing about them and was convinced it was their bloody footprints on the tablecloth in the back room of Madame Phoebe's store.

131

After writing the information on DePaulo on the index cards and posting them in their appropriate positions on the board. I turned my attention to Amy Conterri.

Amy Conterri is an enigma to me. I knew next to nothing about her. That's where I had to start. I knew she had the means and most likely the opportunity to murder Arthur Friedman, but did she have motive. That's what I needed to find out.

I placed another call to Detective Wilder and got his voice mail. I left a message asking him to call me with the names of DePaulo's two associates and asking him to lean on DePaulo hard and fast.

I hung up the phone totally satisfied with my afternoon's work and spent a few minutes studying the display board with all the index cards posted on them. Sometimes seeing things visually in a more logical order makes more sense.

After an hour of studying the cards, I gave up in frustration. Needing a break, I folded the display board and hid it behind the couch in my den. Then I put the dogs on their leashes and headed out for a walk.

The sun was out, but the temperature had dropped to about thirty degrees. Shivering, I urged the dogs into a trot to warm up.

We walked up Sass Road to Twenty-Four Mile Road. After crossing the street, I let the dogs off their leashes and they scampered off into the woods to explore with me following at a more leisurely pace.

I let the dogs run and play for as long as I could without turning into a Popsicle, then called the dogs and put them back on their leashes for the walk home.

I found Lilly bustling around the kitchen preparing dinner when we returned.

"Hi Savannah. Did you have a good day?" she said cheerfully.

"It was okay. How was yours?" I asked, taking a seat at the snack bar.

"Busy. I spent the day at Jackson's apartment rearranging the furniture the movers brought," She answered as she deftly sliced some fresh vegetables for a salad.

"Oh. You should have called. I would've come over and helped you."

"Oh that's okay. I enjoyed it. It's been awhile since Jackson and I spent a day together."

"Well, that's good then. Is Jackson coming over for dinner?" I asked munching on a slice of carrot I'd pilfered from the salad bowl.

"Yes, he should be here any minute."

Just as Lilly finished speaking the doorbell rang. The dogs raced to the door barking wildly.

"I'll get it," I said leaping from my stool.

Sandra stood on the front stoop in tears.

"Sandra! What's wrong?"

"It's Paul," she said between sobs.

"Paul? Come in, honey," I said wrapping my arms around her shoulders and leading her to the couch.

I helped Sandra out of her coat and got her settled. Then sent Lilly scrambling for a box of tissues and a glass of wine for Sandra.

"Tell me what happened?" I asked sitting down next to her on the couch.

"He called and said that his father had been murdered. He was so angry," Sandra said.

"Yes I know. I talked to Detective Wilder this afternoon. What did Paul say?"

"He said that Detective Wilder all but intimated that he'd cut the brake lines on his father's car! Savannah, you know Paul would never do anything like that. He might not have gotten along with his father but he would never kill him," she cried.

Jackson had arrived during Sandra's outburst and sat in one of the chairs listening intently.

"Sandra. I'm sure Detective Wilder was just relaying information to the family. If Paul took it to mean that he was being accused of murder, then maybe he has something to hide," I said, regretting the words as soon as they came tumbling from my mouth. I heard Jackson groan from across the room.

"Savannah! I thought you were my friend. I can't believe you said that! I love Paul and I know he didn't kill his father!" she said, adamantly rising from the couch.

"Sandra, I'm sorry, and I am your friend. I'm not saying he killed his father, I'm just saying that it's possible. It's also very possible that he didn't," I explained.

Sandra sat back down but I knew she wasn't convinced that I believed her.

"Sandra, quite frankly I don't think he killed his father or Madame Phoebe. There were two sets of footprints in Madame Phoebe's store. I know that whoever killed Madame Phoebe killed Arthur Friedman and I know why. But until I can totally clear Paul from any involvement in the murders he will remain a suspect."

"So, you're not working to prove Paul guilty, you're working to prove Paul innocent. You are on his side!" she said brightening.

"Exactly," I said, not daring to look Sandra in the eye.

"Oh, Savannah. I knew I could count on you." she said smiling.

"Of course you can. Now dry your eyes and go fix your make up before dinner is ready," I said giving her a hug.

Sandra obediently rose from the couch and headed into the bathroom with her purse.

"Nice job," Jackson said, giving me a kiss. "You lied through your teeth."

"I didn't lie. I don't think Paul is the killer. But I don't like him and I'm not on his side," I hissed back at him.

"That's my girl," he laughed, patting me on the head.

"Oh shut up," I said, smacking his arm as we headed into the kitchen to help Lilly put dinner on the table.

Sandra joined us at the table and conversation over dinner was light and casual. After dinner we settled in the great room and watched a movie. Sandra and Jackson left together about eleven.

Lilly had already retired to her room so I set the alarm, turned off the lights and went to bed.

Chapter Seventeen

The next morning after grabbing a cup of coffee I headed into my den to call a private detective I'd met in a previous case. He's just starting out so I try to throw some work his way whenever possible.

"Michael Clayton." I heard him answer after the third ring.

"Hi, Michael. It's Savannah Williams. How are you?"

"Hey, Savannah! I'm good. What's up?"

"Listen, do you have time to do a couple of background checks for me?"

"Sure thing. What've you got?" he asked enthusiastically.

I gave Michael all the information I had on Paul Friedman and Amy Conterri.

"I'll get on this right away."

"Thanks, Michael. Talk to you soon."

By the time I got off the telephone, I heard Lilly rustling around in the kitchen making breakfast.

"Morning, Lilly," I said brightly, pouring myself another cup of coffee.

"Morning dear. Sleep well?"

"Like a baby. How about you?"

"Oh I was out like a light. Getting Jackson's apartment together tired me out more than I thought," she answered with a yawn.

"Well, don't overdo," I cautioned.

"I won't. Oh, I'm going to the grocery store today. Anything special you want?"

I rattled off my list of requests while setting the table for breakfast.

After breakfast, I gathered my things and headed over to Madame Phoebe's townhouse to have another look around now that the evidence technicians had finished.

The townhouse still lay in shambles. Although it appeared Amy made an attempt to start the clean up process. The furniture sat upright and the kitchen sat neat and orderly.

I bypassed the first floor and headed straight upstairs. If there was anything of value that's where it would most likely be.

After about an hour or so of thorough searching I'd come up with nothing of interest. Heading back downstairs I noticed a panel in the ceiling.

"Must lead to the attic," I mused out loud.

Never one to leave an attic unexplored, I grabbed the chair from Madame Phoebe's desk and in a few seconds had removed the access panel to the attic.

Too short to hoist myself up, I abandoned the chair in search of a ladder. I found one in the basement along with a flashlight and lugged them up the stairs.

I climbed the ladder and shone the flashlight around the dark attic. Plywood lay over the joists so there would be little problem maneuvering my way around the tiny space. The roof had a high pitch in the center, but for the most part, I was going to have to crawl.

The attic was partially filled with boxes, old lamps, lampshades, and other assorted junk. Using the flashlight to examine the contents of the attic, the light hit a long white string hanging down from the ceiling. I played the light up the string and saw a light fixture. Excellent. I made my way over to the sting and after pulling on it the attic was bathed in a soft glow.

I took a couple of seconds to scan the contents of the attic and then gingerly crawled my way over to a large trunk in the far left corner. Rising to my knees, I gently lifted the lid.

One by one I began to extract the items of memorabilia that lay nestled neatly in the trunk.

An old high school yearbook caught my eye and I casually began to leaf through it. As I looked at the pictures one caught my eye. It showed a Madame Phoebe and Amy wearing cheerleader uniforms. The caption under the picture said: Phoebe and Amy Conterri, our cheerleading sisters.

Quickly thumbing through the yearbook I saw a picture of either Amy or Phoebe with a handsome young man. Underneath the picture the caption identified Amy Conterri and Arthur Friedman, as the high school sweethearts most likely to get married.

"Wonder what happened there?" I said, carefully setting the yearbook aside.

After digging through miscellaneous memorabilia, I came across an old photo album. The album was bound in faded burgundy leather and the pages were constructed out of heavy black paper. The pictures were glued onto the pages, but someone had thoughtfully written full descriptions and people's names beneath each photograph.

I sat cross-legged on the floor and began to flip through the pages. Midway through the album, I found a group picture. According to the notation, the people in the picture were Rubin and Elenore Fleming, Thomas and Rebecca Markley, Hiram and Nancy Webster, Arthur and

Ginny Friedman, and Amy and Phoebe Conterri. The description said that they were on their yearly vacation in Southern California.

"Now that's interesting," I said in surprise.

I quickly skimmed through the album, but found no other pictures of them together. Not wanting to disturb the album, I made the decision to just take the whole thing with me.

I carefully replaced all the items back in the trunk and with the yearbook and photo album in hand, scampered back down the ladder sliding the ceiling panel back into place.

After replacing the ladder and flashlight in the basement, I loaded my finds into my Jeep and left.

After stopping by my office and locking the photo album in my safe, I needed time to figure out where this new information fit into the puzzle, I decided to take a long ride. Generally that helps me clear my head.

I drove up Gratiot Avenue towards Port Huron. Miles of open road lay ahead of me, with the exception of a few charming, historical towns that dotted the roadside here and there.

Less than an hour later, I pulled into the parking lot of a small beach on Lake Huron. I'd come to this beach a lot as a kid, mostly when I needed to think, and must have ended up here instinctively.

A stiff wind greeted me as I left the shelter of the trees and wandered onto the beach. Being early November, the beach was totally deserted. I'd forgotten a coat, and the cool fall air coming in over the water had me shivering in no time, but the air smelled fresh, and the roar of the waves crashing against the shore thundered through my head. Which probably explains why I didn't hear the gunshot, but felt the bullet rip into my left arm causing a searing pain to shoot through my body. I grabbed my arm and felt something sticky on my hand. Looking at my hand I saw blood seeping through my fingers. I grabbed for my gun, but remembered at the last minute I'd left it in my bag in the car.

Crouching down to make myself as small a target as possible, I scanned the area to see where the shot came from.

I heard the faint sound of another shot and flattened my body against the ground. The bullet impacted itself into the sand a couple feet in front of me.

Looking in the direction of the shot, the sun glinted off something by one of the many trees that separated the beach area from the picnic area.

The beach area is totally open and with no cover within easy reach, my only choice was to go for a swim.

In one swift movement, I leapt to my feet and raced for the water. The icy waves battered against my legs and with one deep breath, I dove into the murky depths of the frigid water. The impact of the cold water on my gunshot wound took my breath away.

Swimming out and to the left away from the gunman, I surfaced, gasping for air. Treading water, I scanned the landscape of the beach looking for any sign of movement.

Knowing I couldn't stay in the cold water for more than fifteen minutes without suffering the effects of hypothermia, I quickly dove back underwater and headed toward the backyard of one of the beachfront houses next to the public beach.

I stayed underwater as long as possible, hoping that the gunman would loose sight of me in the rough surf. The sweatshirt I wore, when wet, acted like a weight and kept trying to pull me down into the deep water of the lake.

After what seemed like an eternity, I scrambled to my feet and trudged out of the water into the yard of someone's house, collapsing in the sand behind the safety of a large tree.

Cautiously, rising to my feet and peering around the tree, I realized I was out of visual range of the gunman. Darting from tree to tree towards the front of the house I could see my Jeep sitting in the parking lot. No other cars were in sight. The wind whipped through my wet clothing making my whole body quake violently. My feet and fingers were numb, but I reached into my jean pocket, relieved to see I hadn't lost my car keys in the water. Cupping my keys in my hand, and taking a quick breath, I dashed from behind the tree and sprinted the hundred feet or so to my car.

Shivering, I fumbled with the keys and finally got the door unlocked, crawling into my truck and starting the engine to get some heat.

I fished around in my bag and located my gun and my cell phone. The pain from my left arm became more intense and I felt nauseous and dizzy.

I dialed 911.

"911 operator. What is the nature of your emergency?" A man's voice asked.

"I've been shot. Beach on Wilson Street. Black Jeep," I gasped.

Chapter Eighteen

I woke in a dimly lit room. A wave of nausea washed through my body as I tried to sit up, and my head felt like a herd of elephants were stampeding through it.

A soothing female voice penetrated the pain and gentle hands eased me back down to the pillow. "It's okay, Ms. Williams. Just relax. You're at Lake General Hospital. I'm your nurse, Greta. You just got out of surgery. The doctor said you're going to be fine."

Fighting my way back into consciousness, I slowly opened my eyes. An older nurse in a crisp white uniform stood attentively next to the bed.

"How did I... What happened?" I whispered, trying desperately to recall how I'd ended up here.

"You were shot. Don't you remember? The police found you in your car at the beach. You'd called 911," she answered.

I closed my eyes and forced myself to remember what happened. "My arm. I was shot in the arm."

"Yes. Now just relax. I'm going to go tell the doctor you're awake. Oh, and the police are waiting to talk to you as well as some of your friends. You're quite a popular young lady," The nurse said, adjusting my blankets before bustling out of the room.

She returned a few minutes later with the doctor in tow who introduced himself as Dr. Hart and launched into a ten-minute lecture explaining in excruciating detail the procedure he used to extract the bullet from my arm.

"So when can I go home?" I asked when he'd finished.

"A day or two. You lost a lot of blood and are suffering from a slight case of hypothermia. The police need to talk to you, are you up for it?" he asked.

"Sure, but can I get something to eat? I'm really hungry," I said.

"I'll see what I can do," he smiled.

A few minutes later the nurse returned with a tray of blah looking, foul smelling food and Detective Zeno from the local police department. I related my story in between bites.

"So, what you're saying is you were shot by someone related to the case you're working on?" he asked.

"Yes, exactly. If you don't mind, could you possibly forward the bullet recovered from my arm to Detective Brent Wilder of the Mt. Clements Police Department? I'm curious to see if it came from the same gun used in one of the murders I'm investigating," I said.

"I'll give him a call and arrange it," he answered.

"Thanks. Who else is out there?" I asked, hearing voices outside the door.

"Detective Hathaway from the Ashley Police Department and a delightful woman named Lilly," he chuckled.

"Oh no! Lilly is here!" I cried.

"Boy is she ever. In fact, I better let her get in here to see you before she tears down the hospital to get to you," he laughed.

"Gee, thanks. I thought your job is to serve and protect and you're going to leave me here injured and defenseless to face her alone?" I teased.

"Talk to you later, Ms. Williams. Be careful," he said, walking out of the room.

I eased back against the pillows and closed my eyes. My arm felt like lead and throbbed painfully. At least the pounding in my head finally stopped, and I could think clearly again.

"Savannah! You could have been killed! What were you thinking wandering around a deserted beach by yourself?" Lilly demanded as she burst through the door like a charging bull.

"Mother, please," Jackson pleaded as he came in behind her.

"Don't you Mother please me, Jackson Franklin Hathaway. Someone has to talk some sense into Savannah before she gets herself killed!" she snapped at him.

"Lilly, really, I'm going to be fine. The doctor said so. Please don't yell at me," I whimpered, my eyes filling up with tears.

"Don't cry, Savannah. I'm sorry. It's just that I was so scared. The police called and said you'd been shot were in emergency surgery. I didn't know what to think," Lilly said, rushing to my bedside and giving me a motherly hug.

"It's okay, Lilly," I said.

"I packed you an overnight bag, dear," Lilly said, setting a small duffel bag down on the nightstand.

"Thanks, Lilly," I smiled.

"I don't know what I would do if I lost you," Jackson said, bending down and giving me a gentle kiss.

"I love you, too," I whispered, taking his hand.

We sat and chatted, Jackson on one side holding my hand and Lilly on the other. I knew for the first time in a long time what it really meant to be a family. I didn't realize until now how much I'd missed that.

"Where's my truck?" I asked.

"Still at the beach. According to Detective Zeno the crime lab won't be finished with it until sometime tonight. I'll get someone to drive me back up here tomorrow to pick it up," Jackson explained.

"Oh, okay," I said, yawning.

"We better let Savannah get some rest. Besides, the dogs and Max are going to be wanting their dinner," Lilly said.

"See you tomorrow," Jackson said, kissing me good-bye.

"Night," I answered.

The nurse returned to the room shortly after Jackson and Lilly left to administer a pain shot, for which I was extremely grateful. Within a few minutes I fell into a dreamless, drug induced sleep.

Chapter Nineteen

I woke up at three in the morning with only one thing on my mind; getting out.

After easing the IV out of my arm, I slowly sat up on the edge of the bed. Good, no dizziness. Tentatively getting to my feet, I quietly shuffled around the room and located my bag. My keys were missing, but I carried a spare set of all my keys in a hidden compartment in my bag.

I spent a few more minutes searching for my clothes, but couldn't find them. Then I remembered the overnight bag Lilly brought.

"Thanks, Lilly," I whispered, digging into the duffel to find some clothes.

Quickly getting dressed, I boldly walked down to the nurse's station and informed them that I was checking myself out and could someone please call a taxi. An hour later, after being checked out by a doctor, I leaped into the waiting taxi and told the driver to take me to the beach.

The inside of my truck was soaked in blood, so I grabbed the blanket I always keep in my truck in case of emergency and draped it over the seat before driving off.

I made it to my office by five, started a pot of coffee, and began to write down everything I could remember about the previous day.

At precisely seven o'clock I heard a light knock on the outer office door.

"Got coffee?" Detective Wilder said with a goofy grin.

"Sure do!" I exclaimed. "What are you doing here?"

"I was on my way to work and saw your lights on. Thought I'd stop by," he answered, pouring a cup of coffee and flopping into one of the chairs across from my desk.

"Bull. The Mt. Clements Police Department has a residency requirement and last time I checked Ashley is still ten miles outside Mt. Clements' city limits," I teased.

"Okay, you caught me. I heard you checked yourself out of the hospital and I came by to check on you. Shouldn't you be home resting?"

"I feel fine," I lied. My arm was throbbing horribly.

"If you say so. Now tell me what happened."

As Detective Wilder took notes in that blasted little black notebook of his, I quickly recounted the events of the previous day.

"So you didn't even get a glimpse of who shot you?"

"Not a one. But I'm curious to see if the bullet the coroner recovered from Madame Phoebe matches the one the doctor pulled out of me yesterday. A Detective Zeno is supposed to be getting in touch with you," I replied.

"Done. The bullet is already in the ballistic lab as we speak awaiting testing. He called me yesterday afternoon and I sent someone to pick it up."

"Good. So anything else new?" I asked.

"As a matter of fact there is," he replied.

I waited patiently while he flipped through the pages of his notebook.

"Ah, here it is," he said. "DePaulo's two associates are named Scott Jacobs and Justin Carter. Names mean anything to you?"

"Wait! Scott Jacobs. Isn't that the name of the man who accidentally shot Thomas Markley?" I asked.

147

"What!" he exclaimed, sitting upright in his chair so quickly that he almost knocked over his coffee.

"Oh, I didn't tell you about that?" I said.

"Evidently not. I have no clue what you're talking about," he said.

"Oh, well, sit back and relax, you're going to love this," I smiled.

I quickly filled in him on the accidental shooting of Thomas Markley.

"Wow, so you're thinking maybe Markley's death wasn't such an accident after all," he said when I'd finished.

"Maybe, maybe not, but at any rate Scott Jacobs was never charged. The shooting was ruled an accident according to Mrs. Markley."

"Hmm, I think I'll place a call or two and track down that file. Might make for some interesting reading," he mused.

"It might at that. Can you do me another favor?" I asked.

"Sure, what?"

"Can you obtain some home phone and cell phone records from a week before Arthur Friedman's death to yesterday for me?" I asked.

"Absolutely. Whose do you want?" he said pen poised over his notebook.

"Amy Conterri's, Paul Friedman's, and DePaulo's," I answered.

"So basically everybody on the suspect list," He laughed.

"Exactly." I smiled.

"No problem. What are you looking for?" he asked snapping his notebook shut.

"I'm not really sure, a connection maybe?" I sighed.

"I get it. You're thinking that whoever killed Arthur Friedman and Madame Phoebe didn't work alone," he said.

"It's possible. Something just doesn't feel right. We're missing something," I answered.

"Consider it done. Oh, I got the results back from those footprints on the tablecloth from Madame Phoebe's store," he said.

"And?"

"One comes from a men's size twelve hiking boot, Outdoorsman is the brand name, the other one is from a size ten dress shoe, we're still working to identify the brand," he answered.

"Thanks. Oh, get this, Arthur Friedman and Amy were a big item back in high school," I said, while jotting down the information he'd just given me.

"This case just gets weirder and weirder," he said, shaking his head.

"I know," I agreed.

"Okay, I've got to get to work. I'm going to run Scott Jacobs and Justin Carter through the computer. I'll have a messenger get those phone records to you as soon as I can," he said rising from his chair.

"Great. Thanks," I said, walking him to the door.

"Oh, and Savannah, be careful," he said bounding down the stairs toward his car.

"Definitely," I murmured, shutting the door behind him.

The telephone rang off the hook after Detective Wilder left, but I let the answering machine pick up. I wasn't in the mood to be chastised.

I arranged to have a rental car dropped off. Then called a car detailing shop to come pick up my Jeep so they could clean the interior.

After spending a considerable amount of time thinking and staring out the office window at the light snow falling, I finally decided on a plan of action. After placing a quick phone call I drove into Mt. Clements.

The two-story home of Arthur and Virginia Friedman with its wrap around covered porch and graceful pillars sat on a large lot just outside of the downtown area. The Hunter green clapboard house with pretty white shutters at the windows sat nestled in the center of the lot and surrounded by large old oak trees.

I climbed the four steps to the front door and rang the doorbell, its chime echoed through the house.

A moment or two later an older, but extremely well-groomed woman with silver hair and deep set green eyes, opened the door.

"Ms. Williams?" she asked in a soft, but strong voice.

"Yes. Thank you for seeing me, Mrs. Friedman," I answered.

"My pleasure, please come in," she said, stepping aside graciously to allow me to enter.

I followed her into a large room off the foyer. A comfortable looking dark green and beige plaid sofa and two matching high-back chairs resided by the fireplace. A beautiful oriental rug lay between the chairs and the sofa and an Ethan Allen dark wood coffee table rested on the rug. A window seat occupied the front bay window and held large pillows of solid green and beige complimenting the furniture. Several small tables and lamps lined the room, and many beautiful pieces of art hung on the walls.

"Please, sit down," Mrs. Friedman said, motioning me into one of the chairs. She settled herself on the sofa.

"This room is gorgeous," I said, my eyes still taking in the various pieces of artwork.

"Thank you. Now what may I help you with?" she asked.

"First, I'm terribly sorry for your loss," I began. "As I told you over the phone, I'm working with the Mt. Clements Police Department to find out who is responsible for your husband's death as well as the death of Phoebe Conterri. I'm hoping, if it's not too difficult for you, that you could answer a few questions."

"I can try," she answered, leaning forward.

"Great. Now, as I understand it, you knew Rubin Fleming, Thomas Markley, and Hiram Walker. Is that correct?" I asked.

"Yes. I met Rubin and Hiram in college, along with my husband of course," she said, smiling at some long lost memory.

"What about Thomas Markley?" I asked.

"Oh, I didn't meet Thomas until long after college. He was a friend of Arthurs. They were in the same regiment in the war," she explained.

"And all the families vacationed together?"

"Most of the time yes, unless Rubin was off on a dig somewhere. In that case, Eleanor and the children would join us. Oh, we had some marvelous times," she answered.

"I see. Okay. Now, what about Amy and Phoebe Conterri?"

"Oh, Arthur knew them in high school. He and Amy were quite serious at one time from what I understand."

"Right. What happened there?" I asked.

"I don't really know for sure. Arthur told me that Amy and him split up when they went to separate colleges. I know he remained friends with them both up until he died."

"Didn't that bother you?" I said.

"Phoebe didn't, she was such a sweet soul; so kind and gentle. But, Amy, well, that's another story. I remember when Arthur got the job running the museum and we moved here. Amy would make up excuses to drop by the museum to see Arthur and took every chance she could to integrate herself into our lives. Arthur and I had many and argument over that woman," she said, her eyes flashing with anger.

"What about the relationship between Amy and Phoebe?" I asked.

"Well, they never really got along from what Arthur told me. Everyone gravitated to Phoebe's gentle nature and I think Amy was jealous of her."

"I see. Now, about Arthur and Paul, how did they get along?" I said.

"Oh, Paul and Arthur were inseparable. They did everything together, at least until Paul finished college and started to work at the museum. Then things changed," She said, looking down to examine her fingernails.

"In what way?" I prodded.

"Oh, Paul came back from college with all these grandiose ideas on how to improve the museum and generate more revenue. But Arthur wouldn't hear of it. He said the museum is fine the way it is. Arthur would call Paul arrogant and foolish, and Paul would call Arthur an old man and say he was too embroiled in the past and not willing to keep up with the times," she sighed, a stray tear running down her face which she quickly wiped away with the back of her hand.

"That must have been hard on all of you," I sympathized.

"It was, but especially Paul. They had an argument about the museum the night before Arthur died," she said.

"Really?"

"Yes. Paul got so angry he stormed out of the house to go for a jog, saying that he couldn't wait until his Dad was out of the museum and he could run it," she said, starting to sob.

"I'm sure he didn't mean it. We all say things in anger that we don't really mean," I said, trying to comfort her.

"Yes, I suppose we do," she said, regaining her composure. "But then Arthur died the next day. Poor Paul, he tried so hard to be strong, but I could tell he was devastated."

"I'm sure," I mumbled politely. "Tell me about Arthur."

"Well, Arthur was kind, but very set in his ways. I used to call him an old stick in the mud," she giggled. "He was very conscientious in his work and loved the museum. He was a wonderful husband and a good father.

"Did you notice anything unusual about him the last few weeks before he died?" I asked.

"Well, he did seem quite agitated about something now that you mention it. I tried to talk to him about it several times, but he told me not to worry, that everything would be fine. I assumed he was referring to the budget, but now I'm not so sure," she said, fidgeting with one of the pillows on the sofa.

"Go on," I urged.

"Personally I think it had something to do with that damn crystal skull. I told Arthur not to buy it. It's been nothing but a curse to everyone who's owned it," she spat.

"Why do you say that?"

"Well, everyone who owned it is dead, Ms. Williams," she replied, raising a perfectly plucked eyebrow.

"Yes, but Rubin Fleming and Hiram Walker died of natural causes, Mrs. Friedman," I answered.

"True, but Thomas Markley, Arthur and now Madame Phoebe were all murdered because of that skull," she said.

"Hmm, I was told Thomas Markley died in a hunting accident," I said.

"That's the official version, but if you ask me he was murdered," she affirmed.

"Well, that's definitely a possibility," I agreed. "So you feel Arthur was murdered for the skull then?"

"Definitely," she stated.

"Who do you think killed Arthur?" I asked.

"Well, it wasn't Paul. I can tell you that much," she stated emphatically. "But if I had to guess I would say DePaulo."

"Why?"

"Have you met him?" She asked.

"Yes, I have. On several occasions."

"Well, then you know what I mean. He's unscrupulous and will stop at nothing to get what he wants," she alleged.

"You may be right, Mrs. Friedman. Anyway, I've taken up too much of your time. Thank you for seeing me," I said, rising from my chair.

"You're welcome, Ms. Williams, please let me know if I can help in anyway. I want my husband's killer caught," she stated, walking me to the door.

"So do I, Mrs. Friedman," I said, leaving the house.

Arriving back at my office, I found two manila envelopes lying on the floor inside the door - one from Detective Wilder and one from Michael Clayton. After grabbing a diet Coke from the refrigerator, I settled back in my chair for a good afternoon of reading.

Chapter Twenty

I opened the envelope from Michael Clayton first. It contained the background checks on Amy Conterri and Paul Friedman.

The documents on Paul Friedman showed that, while not wealthy by any means, he enjoyed good credit and paid his bills on time. In fact, the only flaw on his otherwise perfect record was a parking ticket six years ago. He'd graduated Notre Dame University with honors and majored in art history with a minor in business administration.

The documents on Amy Conterri painted quite a picture; she seemed to be in excellent financial condition, having received some money from her grandfather's estate.

Yet something just didn't seem right.

I dialed Michael Clayton's telephone number.

"Michael Clayton," he answered.

"Michael. It's Savannah. Listen, about the documents you dropped off on Amy Conterri, are you sure they're accurate?" I asked.

"Positive, but I can go to the Probate Court and pull the trust documents if you'd like," he answered.

"Please, and while you're there can you get me a copy of the probate file on Phoebe Conterri and Arthur Friedman?"

"Sure thing. I'll have them to you in a couple hours."

"Thanks, Michael. See you then," I said and rang off.

After sorting all the documents and placing them in file folders, I turned my attention to the envelope from Detective Wilder.

It contained the telephone records I'd requested earlier and a copy of the investigation file for Madame Phoebe's murder.

I began to peruse the case file.

The Coroner recovered the bullet from Madame Phoebe's body, but the police still hadn't recovered the murder weapon.

A lot of fingerprints were recovered at Madame Phoebe's store, but that was to be expected. I did note that none of the prints belonged to DePaulo or his henchmen. Not a real surprise; they were pros. They would have worn gloves. Amy Conterri's prints were found in the store, but that meant nothing either.

Not gleaning any other useful information from the file, I turned my attention to the telephone records. These proved to be a lot more interesting.

According to the records, a flurry of activity occurred between DePaulo's suite at the hotel and Amy Conterri the day before and the day after Arthur Friedman's death and again the day after Phoebe's death.

The record also indicated that a few calls from DePaulo's suite were placed to Arthur Friedman both at his home and the museum two days before Arthur Friedman died.

Amy Conterri's telephone records also told an interesting tale. She'd placed three calls to the museum the week Arthur Friedman died. The last call she'd placed to Phoebe took place a week before Phoebe's murder.

I made separate file folders for all the records and put them in my safe. The outer office door opened just as I sat back down.

"Hey, Savannah. I got those records," Michael Clayton said, his long, lanky body striding into my office.

"Thanks, I really appreciate this," I said, taking the file of papers.

"No problem. You need anything else?"

"Not at the moment, but I'll let you know. Send me a bill for what you've done so far."

"Sure thing. See you later," he said as he left.

The probate documents on Arthur Friedman held no surprises. His entire estate he'd left to his wife. According to the preliminary figures, she would be well taken care of and not want for much.

Madame Phoebe's probate documents showed that she'd left an estate valued at well over a million dollars. Her grandfather's trust left her and Amy the sum of a half a million dollars each. Phoebe more than doubled her money, while Amy had gone through most of her inheritance.

According to Phoebe's will, her entire estate, with the exception of a few charitable contributions, she'd left to the Museum of Natural History. Interesting.

One of the unspoken rules of murder is to follow the money. Nine times out of ten that trail will lead to the killer. But in the matter of Phoebe's murder, I couldn't be sure. I didn't think Phoebe was killed for her estate – but for the diamond hidden in the skull. But either way, money was the motive.

I picked up the phone and dialed Michael Clayton's number. He answered on the third ring.

"Hey, Michael, it's Savannah. Listen, I want you to dig deeper on Amy Conterri."

"No problem. When do you need it?" he asked.

"Yesterday," I said and hung up the phone.

The next telephone call was to the attorney who drew up Phoebe's will. I arranged a meeting then called Detective Wilder to meet me at the attorney's office.

A half hour later I found myself and Detective Wilder seated in a well-appointed office talking to Phoebe's attorney, Jerome Fineburg.

"Thank you for seeing us on such short notice, Mr. Fineburg, and I promise this will only take a few minutes," I said.

"My pleasure, what can I do for you?" he asked, looking from Detective Wilder to myself.

"Did Phoebe Conterri change her will in the last year," I said.

Mr. Fineburg opened a file sitting before him on the desk and leafed through a few papers.

"Yes, she did. I remember now. She came to see me a few weeks ago. She was quite insistent that the will be changed while she waited so she could sign it that day. Since the changes were minor, I was able to accommodate her wishes," he answered.

"I thought so. Do you have a copy of the old will?" I asked.

"Yes, I do," he answered, withdrawing a document from the file.

"Could we have a copy of that, please," Detective Wilder asked.

"Of course. Excuse me," Mr. Fineburg replied. He left the office for a few minutes and returned with a copy of Phoebe's old will for myself and Detective Wilder.

According to the document, Amy Conterri was to have inherited the entire estate.

"So, Phoebe Conterri changed her will to state that the Museum of Natural History was to get her entire estate, with the exception of the other charitable contributions?" I asked.

"Yes," Mr. Fineburg confirmed.

"Did Phoebe give you a reason for the change?" Detective Wilder asked.

"No, I'm sorry, she didn't."

"Thank you for your time, Mr. Fineburg. Oh, just one more question," I said, rising from my chair.

"Yes," he said.

"Who opened the estate in the Probate Court upon Phoebe's death?"

"I did. I heard about her death on the news. Since I'm the executor of the estate, it's my duty to open the file. I expect to be distributing the funds within the next week or so," he explained.

"Thank you," I answered and walked outside with Detective Wilder.

After our good-byes, I headed back to the office. While arranging the file, I noticed that Phoebe's estate also included a life insurance policy.

"I wonder who the beneficiary is?" I asked myself.

Without hesitation I picked up the phone and dialed the insurance company's telephone number listed in the probate file. After being transferred four times, I finally reached an insurance adjuster named Pamela.

"You're calling on Phoebe Conterri?" she asked.

"Yes, as I'm sure you're aware, Ms. Conterri died a week or so ago. I'm wondering who the beneficiary is on her life insurance policy," I answered.

"And you're interest in this matter would be?" she asked.

"My name's Savannah Williams. I'm a criminal profiler and a private detective. I've been hired by the Mt. Clements' Police Department to assist in tracking down Phoebe Conterri's killer," I explained.

"Oh, Ms. Williams. I was going to contact you today. We just got this file in."

"Contact me? Why?" I asked.

"You're the named beneficiary on Phoebe Conterri's insurance policy. We need to make arrangements for the payoff. We're sorry for the delay, but the file's been down in our update department. It took a couple of days for me to locate it," she apologized.

"Whoa. Wait. I'm the beneficiary?" I exclaimed.

"Yes."

"The update department?" I asked.

"Yes, you see, Ms. Conterri requested the change in beneficiary a few days before her death. The update department had the file to make the requested change," she explained.

"I see. May I ask the amount of the policy?"

"One million dollars," she stated.

"A million dollars! Are you sure?" I asked.

"Oh, quite sure. Ms. Conterri bought this policy some years ago," she answered.

"Can I ask who the named beneficiary was before?"

"Well... Can you hold for one moment?" she asked.

"Sure," I said, and immediately placed on hold.

"I'm back. Sorry," she said, a few minutes later.

"Look, Pamela, I need that name. Now, I can either have the Mt. Clements' Police Department subpoena that file, or you can save us both a lot of time just tell me. Either way, I'm going to find out," I said.

"That won't be necessary. I just called the Mt. Clements Police Department and verified you are acting in an official capacity. Actually there were joint beneficiaries - her sister, Amy Conterri, and her nephew, Scott Jacobs. They were to split the money equally," she said.

"Oh my dear God," I whispered.

"Ms. Williams, are you okay?"

"Yes, yes, I'm fine. Does Amy Conterri and Scott Jacobs know they're not the beneficiaries?" I asked.

"They will by this afternoon. I have a message that Amy Conterri called this morning, but I was in a meeting and haven't had time to return her call."

"Could you please make a copy of the entire file and overnight it to Detective Brent Wilder, of the Mt. Clements Police Department? I'll give you the address."

"Of course. Now, there's also some paperwork I need your signature on in order to issue your check. Since we're local, I'd like to meet with you tomorrow to obtain you're signature and close out the file. Where can I meet you?"

I gave her the addresses for both my office and Detective Wilder's.

"Okay, so tomorrow around ten?" she asked.

"That's fine. Now, Pamela, you aren't going to tell them that I'm the beneficiary are you?" I asked.

"Oh, of course not. I'd be fired," she answered.

"Thanks for your help," I said, hanging up the phone in a daze. So many thoughts were racing through my head I couldn't even begin to sort them out. Plus the throbbing in my arm had intensified to outrageous proportions.

"A walk. I need a walk. And drugs. I definitely need some drugs," I mumbled, easing into my coat.

I trudged through the freshly fallen snow to the drug store down the street from my office. The drug store is a warm, friendly place. Every time I go in there I feel like I've walked into the drugstore in Mayberry, from the old Andy Griffith show. An old-fashioned soda counter sits off to the left of the front door. The worn wooden floors slope at different angles depending on where you stand, and are probably original to the building. An older couple, Fred and Martha Burns, own the store. Fred is at least sixty-five with a balding head and bulbous nose. But his green eyes and sharp ears don't miss much. Martha, a small, but stout woman, wears her silver hair in a short, easy to care for style, and definitely has her finger on the pulse of the community. There isn't much that can go on around here without her knowing about it.

"Hey, Savannah," Fred greeted me with a friendly wave from behind the pharmacy counter.

"Hi, Fred. Can you fill these for me?" I asked, handing him the prescriptions for pain medication and antibiotics the doctor gave me.

"Sure thing. Just be a minute. What happened? This is pretty strong stuff," he said, reading the prescriptions.

"A metal tubular object fired out of a device used to shoot such projectiles caught me in the upper limb yesterday," I responded with a wink. Fred and I have played this game for years.

"Ahh, you got shot in the arm," he said, after thinking for a second.

"Occupational hazard," I shrugged, sitting down on one of the stools at the soda counter.

"You need to be more careful," Martha scolded, having joined us from the other side of the store.

"I know," I sighed. I watched her pour me a steaming cup of hot chocolate and drop in a handful of those mini marshmallows I loved so much.

"Drink this. It'll make you feel better," she said, placing the steaming mug before me.

Martha is a firm believer that there wasn't an ailment in the world a mug of her hot chocolate couldn't cure.

"Thanks," I said, gratefully taking a sip.

"You don't seem yourself today, Savannah. Something else wrong?" she asked.

"Oh, its this case I'm working on. It's just giving me fits," I grumbled.

"The Phoebe Conterri murder," she nodded.

"How'd you know I'm working on that case?" I asked.

"My dear, this is a small town. People talk. You know that."

"True," I nodded. "What people?"

"Well, Phoebe's sister, Amy, was in here a few days ago with a young man. They sat right there," she said pointing to two unoccupied stools at the end of the counter.

"How do you know Amy Conterri?" I asked.

"Oh, she's been coming in here for years," Fred yelled from the pharmacy.

"Really. Go on," I urged.

"Anyway," Martha said, handing me a spoon so I could scoop the marshmallows out of my mug. "I didn't hear too much of what they were saying. It was a Saturday afternoon, and you know how busy we are on Saturday. But, I did hear your name mentioned a couple of times as I passed by them."

"How were they acting?"

"Nervous. Kind of fidgety, you know. Kept glancing around to make sure they weren't overheard," Fred said, handing me my prescriptions.

"Exactly, and I think they were having an argument," Martha nodded her head in agreement.

"What makes you think that?" I asked.

"By the looks on their faces. The young man seemed upset with Amy," Martha said.

"This man Amy Conterri was with, can you describe him?" I asked.

"Kind of a young fella, couldn't be more than twenty-two or so. Dark hair and eyes," Fred began.

"Yes, and not dressed for the weather. I remember it was cold that day because I had to dig out a warm sweater to wear," Martha said.

"Yes, that's right. You wore that blue one I like so much because it matches your eyes," Fred agreed.

"Oh hush, Fred. This is serious," Martha blushed. "I remember he was wearing a pair of jeans, not the faded ones mind you, but they were dark blue, like they were a new pair he was wearing for the first time. They looked a little stiff. Oh, and a dark green T-shirt, plain, not the kind with the pocket on the front."

"And a black leather jacket, not the kind them motorcycle riders wear, but more like a bomber jacket. I remember, because I complimented him on it. I've wanted one of those for years. Reminds me of the one I wore in the war," Fred added.

"I never knew you wanted one of those? Well, Christmas is coming now isn't it," Martha said with a wink.

"Isn't she the greatest?" Fred said, giving Martha a quick hug.

"Yes, she is. Now back to the man. Anything else you remember?" I asked.

"His shoes. I remember thinking as he left that at least he wore sensible shoes," Martha said, wrinkling her forehead up in thought.

"What kind of shoes?"

"Not shoes, boots really. Like those hiking boots they sell everywhere. The only reason I noticed them at all is because of how heavy they sounded when he walked," Martha explained.

"Oh, and there was that other man asking about Savannah a few weeks back. Remember him, Martha? That funny little man," Fred said.

"Funny little man?" I asked.

"Yes, I remember him now that you mention it, Fred," Martha said.

"Who are you two talking about?" I asked. While I loved Fred and Martha dearly, they could sometimes make my head spin.

"That funny little man. He was in here about a month ago. I think he's foreign," Martha said.

"Kind of short, clipped accent, dark complexioned, perfectly groomed? Wears a black cape and expensive suits?" I said.

"Yes, that's him! So you do know him," Martha exclaimed.

"I know him. His names' Viktor DePaulo, and he's an art and antiquities dealer. What did he want?" I inquired.

"He said he needed to hire a private investigator to find something for him. He said he'd seen your sign and asked if you were any good," Fred said.

"Of course we told him you were the best," Martha beamed.

"Thanks. What else did he ask?"

"Oh, he asked all about you. I can't remember exactly, it's been awhile," Martha said, disappointed.

"Course we didn't tell him much, him being a stranger and all," Fred assured me.

"I appreciate that," I said.

"Well, you know Martha and I think of you as one of our own," Fred said.

"I know. Just don't go changing your life insurance policies, okay?" I joked.

"What?" They asked in unison.

"Never mind. Bad joke. Anyway, I need to be getting home. Lilly will kill me if I'm late for dinner," I smiled.

"Oh, how is Lilly? She's such a dear soul. Comes in here all the time," Martha said.

"Always has time for a cup of tea and a good chat, too," Fred added.

"Lilly's fine. I'll tell her you said hello," I assured them.

"Don't you go and take those pills until you're in for the night," Fred cautioned. "They'll knock you for a loop."

"I won't. Thanks, Fred," I said, paying my bill. "See you two later."

<u>So, DePaulo was asking about me. Isn't that curious?</u> I thought, stuffing my hands deep inside my coat pockets as I plodded through the snow to my office. I hung up my coat and poured myself a cup of hot coffee.

"What was Madame Phoebe thinking? A million dollars! What the hell am I supposed to do with a million dollars? Well, I know what to do with a million dollars, but that's not the point?" I moaned flopping into my chair and lighting a cigarette. "What do I have to do? Add myself to the suspect list?"

"What the heck are you mumbling about?" Jackson asked, walking into my office. I didn't even hear the door open.

"Madame Phoebe made me the beneficiary of her life insurance policy. I've just inherited a million dollars," I blurted out.

"A million dollars! Are you serious?" he exclaimed.

"I'm afraid so. I'm going to have to pull myself off this case. Talk about a major conflict of interest," I whined.

"I see your point. But, quite frankly, I've never seen anyone so distraught over inheriting a million dollars. Don't you know what this means, Savannah? You'll never have to worry about money again. You've got it made."

"Oh grow up, Jackson. I'm not interested in the money. It's blood money. I wish it'd never happened," I snapped.

"I know. I'm sorry. Come on. I'll follow you home. Mom sent me to fetch you for dinner. She's not real happy with you, you know," he said, helping me into my coat.

"I didn't figure she would be. But I couldn't stand being in that hospital for another second," I said, locking all the paperwork in my safe. "Oh, I have to drop off the rental car and pick up my truck at the auto detailing place up the street first."

"No problem. We'll drop off the car and I'll drive you to get your truck. We better get moving. You know how Mom is if we're late for dinner."

Jackson and I finished my errands and a half-hour later were sitting down to dinner. I wasn't real hungry and just wanted to go to bed. Jackson, on the other hand, couldn't wait to tell Lilly about my inheritance.

"Oh my goodness gracious! What are you going to do with that kind of money?" Lilly asked.

"Invest it I guess. I really haven't given it much thought. I've been so busy today," I answered.

"Well, there's plenty of time to think about it. You look pale and tired, Savannah," Lilly said. "Your arm hurts doesn't it?"

"Yes. In fact, I think I'm going to take a pain pill and go to bed.

"You go ahead. I'll be there in a minute to check on you," Lilly said.

"Okay," I answered and trotted off to my bedroom.

I changed into my nightgown and swallowed a pain pill before crawling under the covers. Rambo and Sydney, sensing I didn't feel well, snuggled up next to me on the bed and Max curled up on one of the pillows and started to purr.

After several minutes I felt the familiar numbness that only occurs when strong painkillers take effect, and drifted off to sleep.

Chapter Twenty-One

The next morning I snuck out of the house before Lilly even woke up for fear that she would make me spend an insufferable day in bed fussing over me. I made it to the office at six and started a pot of coffee. The only thing on my mind was damage control. If the press got wind of my inheriting from Phoebe's estate they'd be all over it like vultures.

I dialed Detective Wilder's cell phone number.

"Detective Wilder," he answered on the first ring.

"Hi, its Savannah. Can you stop by my office on your way in. I need to talk to you."

"On the way. This sounds serious," he replied.

"It is. See you in a few minutes," I said, ringing off.

Ten minutes later Detective Wilder strode into my office and I poured him a cup of coffee.

"So what's up?" he asked, sitting down.

"I need to pull myself off this case. I've got a conflict of interest," I stated.

"What's that?" he asked.

"Madame Phoebe made me her beneficiary on her life insurance policy a few days before she died."

"For how much?"

"A million dollars," I sighed.

"Wow!" he said, letting out a long whistle.

"I know. So, obviously I can't continue to work on this matter," I explained.

"Did you know about this?" he asked.

"Not until yesterday," I said, detailing my conversation with the insurance company.

"I really don't think there's a problem, considering you didn't know about it. But then again we don't want to do anything to blow this case," he answered.

"Exactly."

"Okay, let's do it this way. Officially you're off the case, but unofficially I want you to keep working it. You're the best shot we have at solving this thing," he admitted.

"Thanks. I was hoping you'd say that," I said, relieved.

"So, who was the beneficiary before?"

"Her nephew, Scott Jacobs, and Amy Conterri."

"Wait! Scott Jacobs is her nephew? The same Scott Jacobs who works for DePaulo?" he asked.

"Apparently so. Scott must be Amy's son," I mused.

"Can you prove it?" He asked.

"Not yet, but I have someone working on it. I should know today."

"Okay. Let me know. Oh, I got the ballistics report back on the bullets. The bullet that killed Phoebe Conterri and the bullet they took out of your arm came from different guns," he reported after consulting his little black notebook.

"I figured as much," I replied.

"I think it's about time you issued some search warrants. We've got to find that murder weapon," I suggested.

"You're right. But we've got to execute them simultaneously. Otherwise, there's a chance that weapon could disappear all together."

"So four teams all going in at the same time?"

"Four? I only count three," he asked.

"Four. The museum, Paul Friedman's house, DePaulo's suite, and Amy Conterri's house," I said, ticking them off on my fingers.

"I missed the museum. You really don't think Paul Friedman is involved though, do you,"

"Not really, but we have to be sure," I replied.

"Right."

"You take care of those search warrants, I'm going to go back to the store and Madame Phoebe's house."

"I'll arrange for the warrants this morning and form the teams. We'll serve them at one this afternoon. I'll call you when we're finished," he said, rising to leave. "You know, we could just bring the whole bunch in for questioning."

"Not yet. They know we don't have anything concrete or we would've dragged them into the station days ago. Let them think that just a little bit longer," I smiled slyly.

"Then why take a shot at you?"

"Because the killer knows I'm getting close."

"Are you?" he asked.

"Most definitely," I affirmed.

"Okay. Talk to you later. Oh, and Savannah, stay away from the beach," he joked, walking out of my office.

"So not funny!" I yelled after him.

A few minutes later my door flung open and Sandra came bursting through.

"Savannah! Lilly just told me you got shot! Why didn't you call me?"

"I'm sorry, Sandra. I've just been so busy. I'm fine, really."

"Are you sure?"

"I'm sure! Have I got news for you! But you have to promise not to breathe a word!" I exclaimed.

"I promise. Cross my heart and hope to die," she said, her emerald eyes wide with excitement.

"I mean no one, Sandra," I cautioned.

"Okay, okay, now tell me before I explode!"

"Madame Phoebe made me the beneficiary on her million dollar life insurance policy," I said.

"A million dollars! Oh my God! Savannah!" she cried.

"Shhh. Quiet!" I hushed her.

"Sorry," she said, lowering her voice. "What are you going to do with all that money?"

"I don't have a clue. Invest it I guess," I shrugged.

"Maybe hire a secretary? You've needed one for years," she suggested.

"You're right. I could really use a secretary. And, I could rent the other office suite on this floor and bring Michael Clayton in as a full-time detective. Lord knows he needs the money, and I could use the help," I added.

"Great idea! I knew we'd come up with something. Then you can invest the rest," Sandra said.

"It just all seems so self serving," I sighed.

"Not really. You're using the money to benefit others in the long run. Having another detective on staff will allow you to take on more cases and help more people. Madame Phoebe would approve, Savannah."

"No wonder you're so good at marketing, Sandra. You can justify anything," I teased.

"Just doing my job," she winked.

"So, are you still seeing Paul Friedman?" I asked.

"Yes, we have a date tomorrow night. He's been so busy with the museum since his father died we really haven't seen much of each other lately, although we did manage to squeeze in a quick lunch day before yesterday."

"You must miss him," I sympathized.

"I do. But I've been busy myself trying to get the new marketing campaign off the ground for the museum. Wait until you see the new ads, Savannah, they're awesome, if I do say so myself," she beamed.

"I know they're going to be great, Sandra. You always do such a terrific job."

"Thanks. Anyway, I've got to get to the office. Let's have lunch next week," she suggested.

"Sounds good. Call me. And remember, not a word to anyone about the money," I warned.

"My lips are sealed," she assured me, gathering her things to leave.

"Take care, Sandra," I said, giving her a hug.

"You too, Sweetie, be careful."

Most of the morning I spent on routine correspondence and sorting through the mound of mail that piled up over the last few days. Sandra was right - I did need a secretary. I also wandered downstairs to speak to my landlords about renting the remainder of the second floor of the building and my remodeling plans. We agreed on a fair price, and I signed a lease.

At ten o'clock an attractive young blonde walked through my office door.

"Ms. Williams? Hi, I'm Pamela Davis from the insurance company," she introduced herself.

"Please, sit down. Coffee?" I offered.

"No, thank you. I have some papers I need you to sign and I need to see your driver's license and Social Security card, please," she said, extracting some files from her briefcase.

A few minutes later with all the paperwork concluded, Pamela Davis took her leave, and I had a check in my hand for one million dollars. I wasn't exactly sure how everything happened so quickly, but Pamela assured me all the paperwork was in order, and they would be closing their file.

I drove into Mt. Clements to see the investment broker I'd known for years. After explaining what I wanted to do with some of the money, he issued me some temporary checks, and said he'd be in touch in a few days with an investment strategy. I arrived back at my office around eleven or so.

About a half-hour later Michael Clayton came to drop off the information on Amy Conterri.

"So, fill me in," I said, glancing through the file.

"Twenty-six years ago, Amy Conterri married William Jacobs. Two years later they divorced. Their marriage produced one child, a boy, named Scott. According to the final divorce decree, Amy Jacobs took back her maiden name of Conterri. Amy and William had joint custody of Scott, but he spent most of his time with his mother. I managed to trace William Jacobs, only to discover he died three years ago of a heart attack. Scott Jacobs has lived an interesting life. He graduated high school here in town then went to college in Arizona. I managed to track down some of his old college buddies who told me Scott left college to 'find himself' and they haven't had contact with him since. I know there was a hunting accident in which Scott accidentally shot his employer, Thomas Markley, a jeweler. No charges were filed. Not long after that, Scott hooked up with a man named Viktor DePaulo, an arts and antiquities dealer of questionable business practices. Scott acts as a courier and personal assistant to Mr. DePaulo. That's all I've been able to find out. Want me to keep digging?"

"No. It's pretty much what I thought. I just needed confirmation. Good job. Thanks," I replied.

"You're welcome. Anything else?" he asked.

"Yes, as a matter of fact there is," I said, quickly outlined my idea to bring him on as a full time investigator, offering him a generous salary, and explaining my plans to renovate the second floor.

"Are you serious?" he asked.

"Yes, I thought we'd run a hallway off the reception area down to what will be your office, and add a conference room and file room in the space at the back of the building. What do you think?" I asked.

"It sounds great! When do I start?"

"Right now! I'm putting you in charge of the renovations. Just run everything by me first, okay?"

"I'm all over it. Thanks, Savannah. You have no idea what this means to me," he said on a more serious note.

"I think I do. Now go! We both have work to do," I laughed.

"Later!" he yelled as he fairly ran to the door. I heard him scamper down the stairs and a loud 'Whoohoo' echo between the buildings.

"It's definitely going to be interesting," I chuckled to myself locking up the office. I felt good about my decision to bring Michael on as a full time investigator. What he lacked in field techniques, such as surveillance, he more than made up for in his uncanny ability to ferret out information no one else could find.

Chapter Twenty-Two

I drove over to Madame Phoebe's condominium for another look around. Maybe I'd missed something. I knew Madame Phoebe will enough to know that she would've never changed the beneficiary on her life insurance policy without an explanation. While conducting my search, I couldn't help but think about how scared Madame Phoebe must have been the last few days of life.

"Always put yourself in the shoes of your victim and the mind of the killer," An instructor at Quantico told me once.

Deciding to test that premise, I made myself comfortable on the couch in Madame Phoebe's living room and closed my eyes. Clearing my mind of all outside thoughts, I concentrated only on Madame Phoebe and the events surrounding the crystal skull.

It stood to reason that Arthur Friedman would have either called or visited Madame Phoebe to tell her he'd purchased the crystal skull.

Sometime during that conversation he would've told Madame Phoebe that DePaulo had contacted him. Knowing that the security system at the museum was outdated and ineffective, Arthur Friedman then asked Phoebe to safeguard the skull until he could deal with DePaulo.

Phoebe would've readily agreed, eager to help out an old friend. But she would have suggested that the skull be placed in the hands of someone unconnected with their inner circle to ensure the skulls safety. It's highly doubtful that Phoebe knew about the diamond secreted away in the skull. To Phoebe, the skull would represent an ancient relic with mystical powers. Arthur Friedman agreed to these terms knowing he could trust Phoebe explicitly.

After their meeting, Arthur Friedman either mailed or sent a messenger to drop off the skull to Phoebe, along with the letter he'd written outlining their agreement. A few days later, Arthur Friedman died.

Madame Phoebe, not a stupid woman by any means, would probably figure out Arthur Friedman was murdered and suspect DePaulo. Knowing DePaulo would discover she had the skull and come after her, she then made the decision to send the skull to me, as per her agreement with Arthur Friedman.

"She knew she was going to be murdered," I said, sitting up on the couch. "But she also knew I'd stop at nothing to find out who killed her. She sent me the skull not only for safekeeping, but as a clue. Of course! That's it!"

Leaping off the couch, I started to pace the front room. I always think better when I pace.

"Okay, so she sends me the skull with a cryptic note saying that she'll explain everything when I come by the store. But, the killer gets to her first. But who's the killer? Damn it, Madame Phoebe! Help me here!" I screamed, stomping my foot on the floor in frustration.

The second my foot hit the floor, a framed photograph, one of many hanging on the wall of the stairway leading to the second floor, came crashing to the floor, shattering the glass.

"What the..." I yelped, jumping in fright.

Careful to avoid the broken glass, I picked up the picture. It showed Arthur Friedman and his wife, Paul Friedman, Phoebe, and Amy standing on the side of the museum. Arthur Friedman held a pair of scissors in one hand and a large ribbon in the other. I turned the picture over, removed the back of the frame and slid the picture out. On the back of the picture, written in Phoebe's familiar hand, it said, 'Ribbon cutting ceremony for the new east wing of the Museum, April, 1990.'

"That's strange. Why would Phoebe and Amy be there?" I asked myself.

Without hesitation, I fished my phone out of my bag and dialed Michael Clayton's cell phone number.

"Michael Clayton," he answered.

"Michael, its Savannah. I need you to find out anything you can about the east wing added to the Museum of Natural History in April of 1990," I said, cleaning up the glass from the broken picture.

"Okay. Anything in particular?"

"Yes, I want to know where the money came from."

"Got it. I need a key to the office. I'm meeting a contractor there tomorrow for an estimate. Can I meet you this afternoon?" he asked.

"Sure thing. I'll meet you at the office."

"Cool. Later," he said, and the line went dead.

After cleaning up all the glass, I checked to make sure everything was secure before leaving to drive into Mt. Clements. I wanted another look around Madame Phoebe's store.

I'd just pulled into a parking spot when my cell phone rang.

"Savannah. Hi, it's Detective Wilder. Listen, we've executed the warrants, but came up empty on all counts," he said.

"Damn," I answered. "Where in the hell is the gun?"

"I don't know. But, I do know that DePaulo's men each carry a small weapon, neither of which matches the make or caliber of the murder weapon. We didn't find any other weapons in DePaulo's suite," he said.

"What about the cars? I know DePaulo rides around in a black Lincoln, and there's a black Grand Am, too," I said.

"We searched them. Nothing," he answered.

"Okay. So it looks like we're back to square one," I sighed.

"We'll keep looking. We'll find it," he assured me.

"What are you up to today?"

"I'm at Phoebe's store. I want to take another look around," I said.

"Okay. Call me if you need anything. I'll be here all day," he answered.

"Will do. Bye," I answered and hung up.

I let myself into the store and turned on all the lights. Various boxes, all neatly addressed to different manufacturers, sat in the back room. I spent a lot of time searching through all the boxes. Satisfied that they held nothing of importance, I taped them shut and made sure they were all stacked like I'd found them.

After thoroughly inspecting every nook and cranny of the store, I collapsed in the remains of one of the chintz chairs. I reminisced about the time spent with Madame Phoebe and the conversations we'd had over the years. I could still picture her behind the display cases waiting on customers. Overcome with emotion, I broke down and cried.

"Stop it!" I admonished myself, wiping the tears away with the sleeve of my coat. "This is not going to get you anywhere."

I gathered my things, locked the store, and headed back to my office.

I found Michael waiting patiently outside the door to my office.

"Sorry I'm late. I got tied up," I said.

"No problem. I just got here myself. It took me a while to find the financial information on the east wing of the museum," Michael said, grabbing a beer out of the refrigerator for himself and a pouring a glass of wine for me before making himself comfortable in the chair across from my desk.

"What did you find out?" I asked, sipping my wine.

"Most of the money came from a Federal grant, but there were several private investors. Phoebe and Amy Conterri each contributed two hundred thousand dollars."

"Well, that explains why they were at the ribbon cutting ceremony," I said.

"Want to tell me about the case? Sometimes it helps talking it out," Michael suggested.

After calling Lilly to tell her I was going to be late for dinner, I started at the beginning and took him through the entire case. Michael sat listening intently; his eyes closed and his fingertips pressed together in a pyramid formation.

"Okay," he said when I'd finished. "The way I see it is DePaulo or Amy Conterri is the trigger man."

"Right, but I honestly don't think DePaulo pulled the trigger, but he could have ordered his henchmen to do it. Somehow, I just don't see that either."

"Why?"

"Well. Why kill? The diamond legally belongs to him as far as I can tell. Why not just wait until the diamond surfaces and put his claim in?"

Michael got up and began to pace the room. "Because what if the diamond doesn't surface? I mean, what if DePaulo didn't think anyone else knew about the diamond?"

"No. That doesn't wash. DePaulo isn't a stupid man. Plus, Scott Jacobs, one of DePaulo's associates, worked for Thomas Markley. Isn't it likely he'd have told DePaulo about the location of the diamond?" I asked.

"I see your point. And, I'm sure Scott Jacobs worked out a nice little deal with DePaulo in exchange for that information."

"Exactly," I replied.

"Okay. So DePaulo's our lead suspect then, right?" Michael asked.

"I guess. But I still haven't been able to clear Amy Conterri, yet, either," I sighed.

"True. It's quite a puzzle, I'll give you that," he chuckled, draining his beer.

"Tell me about it," I retorted, walking into the small kitchen to wash out my wine glass.

"Have you heard from DePaulo?" Michael asked, rinsing out his beer bottle.

"Not a peep. He's kept a pretty low profile lately. Maybe its time I paid him a visit."

"Couldn't hurt," he agreed.

Michael and I finished locking up the office and walked down the back stairs to the parking lot. I gave him a key to the office, and we bid each other good night.

Lilly, Sandra, and Jackson greeted me when I walked through the door.

"Hi! What's going on?" I asked, taking off my coat and hanging it on the hook in the laundry room.

"Nothing, just catching up!" Sandra informed me.

"Oh. Sorry I'm late," I said.

We spent a pleasant evening laughing, eating and drinking. I fell into bed around midnight totally exhausted.

Chapter Twenty-Two

I woke up knowing I had to make something happen; and fast. My attempt to draw out the killer only resulted in getting myself shot. Something I didn't want to repeat anytime soon.

After a quick breakfast, I drove to the office only to find Michael and a contractor in an animated discussion about the remodeling project.

"Morning, Boss. I made coffee," Michael greeted me.

"Hi, Michael. You call me boss again and you're a dead man," I teased, walking into the kitchen to grab a cup of coffee.

"Acknowledged," Michael laughed.

I sequestered myself in my office for the next hour or so answering my e-mail, and sorting through the mail. Michael and the contractor left around nine, so I hunkered down to review the case file.

"Hmmm," I thought to myself, walking around the office an hour later to stretch my legs. "Maybe I just rattled their cages the wrong way."

Before I even finished the thought, Amy Conterri burst through the door. She appeared to be extremely upset and visibly shaking.

"Amy!" I exclaimed.

"I want you to find out who the beneficiary is on my sister's life insurance policy," she demanded, her face filled with rage.

"Calm down. Take a seat. Let me get you a glass of water," I offered.

Amy took a deep breath and flung herself into a chair. I rushed off to the kitchen and returned with a glass of water.

"Now, what happened?" I asked.

"Phoebe had a life insurance policy. I called the insurance company and they sent me the paperwork to fill out. I mailed it back along with a copy of her death certificate. When I called them a couple of days ago, they told me that Phoebe changed her beneficiary a day or two before she was killed, but wouldn't tell me who the beneficiary is. I want you to find out," Amy explained.

"How do you know you were the beneficiary in the first place?" I asked.

"Phoebe told me when she purchased the policy," she said, taking a sip of water. I noticed her hands were still shaking.

"Phoebe had every right to change her beneficiary, Amy." It'd taken only a split second to decide to push Amy as hard as I could.

"That's not the point! We're talking about one million dollars," Amy seethed.

"Amy, I'm sorry. There's nothing I can do for you."

"But it's my money!" Amy screamed, leaping to her feet, her hands clenched into tight fists.

"No, Amy, it's not. Besides, weren't you going to have to split the insurance money with your son, Scott?"

"Well, yes, but... Wait! How do you know about Scott? And how do you know Scott and I were the beneficiaries?" she asked, her eyes narrowing.

"The Mt. Clements Police Department hired me as the profiler in this matter," I answered.

"So, you knew all this before I even walked through the door!" she screamed.

"Yes," I said, keeping my voice calm and even.

"Then, you know who the beneficiary is on Phoebe's life insurance policy, don't you?" She asked, placing her hands on the edge of my desk and leaning towards me.

"Yes, as a matter of fact, I do," I confirmed.

"Tell me!" she demanded.

"I can't. It would be a breach of client confidentiality," I explained, shrugging my shoulders.

"I don't care about that! Tell me who stole my one million dollars!" she shrieked.

I rose from my desk and walked past Amy to the reception area. Upon reaching the door to the outside stairway, I opened it and turned to face her.

"Good bye, Ms. Conterri. This meeting is over," I said, meeting her angry glare with one of calm resolve.

Amy grabbed her purse and stomped towards the door.

"I will find out," she hissed, and exited down the stairs. I slammed the door behind her.

"That went well," I laughed, walking back into my office.

After arranging to meet DePaulo around noon, I spent most of the morning on the phone with my broker going over the financial plan he'd developed.

At precisely twelve o'clock, DePaulo strode through the doorway carrying a black briefcase. We exchanged greetings and made ourselves comfortable in my office to get down to the business at hand.

"Mr. DePaulo," I began. "I've spent a considerable amount of time and energy on this matter, and quite frankly, I'm ready to put this whole mess to bed once and for all. I'm hoping you can help me in that regard."

"I will assist in any way I can, Ms. Williams. What is it you require?" he asked.

"Honesty, Mr. DePaulo. Nothing more, nothing less," I answered. Rising, I retrieved two cups of coffee and placed one before him before retaking my position behind my desk.

He raised the cup to his lips and took a small sip, testing for temperature. "I'm sorry, Ms. Williams, you have me at a disadvantage."

"A disadvantage?" I stopped stirring my coffee. "Is honesty a foreign concept to you, Mr. DePaulo?"

He met my steady gaze with a quizzical glance. I could almost hear the wheels spinning in his head, deciding on what tact to take at this juncture of the conversation.

"Not at all, Ms. Williams. Perhaps if you clarified what exactly we are being honest about, I would be better able to assist you," he replied.

"That's fair," I admitted. "Okay, here goes. I know your real name is Viktor Nazareth. The same Viktor Nazareth who owned the Nazareth Diamond Mine where the Star of Angel diamond was found."

DePaulo's face registered a look of surprise, which he quickly checked.

"And I know that your associates shot at me at least once, maybe twice. Whether they did so under your orders or not is immaterial. Speaking of your two employees, I'm sure you're aware that Scott Jacobs is the son of Amy Conterri, and worked for Thomas Markley. You remember Thomas Markley, don't you Mr. DePaulo? He worked in your mine and stole the other half of the Star of Angel's diamond which he later placed in the skull."

The look of total shock on DePaulo's face made me stop.

"Ms. Williams," he stammered, his hands shaking so severely that it took both of them to replace his coffee cup on the desk without spilling it. "I had no idea. Scott Jacobs, are you sure?"

"Positive," I said. Either DePaulo was an incredible actor, or he really didn't know. I believed the latter. "Wait, Scott Jacobs didn't tell you about the diamond?"

"Scott Jacobs told me, Ms. Williams, but not how you think. Part of his job was to track down the whereabouts of the skull. Every few days he'd come up with seemingly new information. I assumed he got the information through research and persistence. But, if what you say is true, and I have no reason to doubt you, he already knew where the skull was," he said, regaining his composure.

"I don't think he knew exactly where the skull was until Arthur Friedman bought it for the museum. After he accidentally shot Thomas Markley in a hunting accident he left town. He just needed to track down the skull from there. I'm sure his plan was to call Mrs. Markley and find out what happened to the skull, but that became unnecessary after he found out I had it," I answered.

"So, that day I came to visit you, what would Scott have done if you'd given me the skull?" he asked.

"My guess is that he would have taken it and disappeared before you had a chance to retrieve the diamond," I said.

DePaulo, absently stroking his mustache with his index finger, sat back in his chair taking a few minutes to digest all this new information. I got up to pour us each another cup of coffee in an effort to buy myself some time to think. DePaulo not knowing about Scott Jacobs put the case in a whole new light.

"Mr. DePaulo," I said, after a few minutes. "I can place Scott Jacobs and Justin Carter in Madame Phoebe's store at or around the time of her death. Their footprints were found in the store. What can you tell me about that?"

Before he could even open his mouth to answer it hit me. I held my hand up to silence him, closing my eyes to allow the thought process follow through.

"Mr. DePaulo," I said, opening my eyes a moment or two later. "I'm afraid I must ask you to leave. I'll be in touch. In the meantime, don't say anything to anyone about what we discussed today; especially Scott Jacobs. You are to treat him the same way you always do. Understood?"

"Well, yes, but I don't understand..." he began.

"I know. Sorry. I'll explain later," I said, leaping to my feet and walking to the door, leaving him no choice but to follow.

"As you wish," he said, taking my hand.

"Good-bye, Mr. DePaulo," I smiled.

"You are a remarkable woman, Ms. Williams. When this matter is resolved, I shall enjoy getting to know you better," he said, brushing his lips over my hand.

I shut the door behind him and raced to dial the telephone.

"Detective Wilder, its Savannah. I need you at my office now," I said.

"What's up?" he asked.

"Just get here and bring the photos from the crime scene with you!" I exclaimed.

"On the way," he said.

Ten minutes later, Detective Wilder burst through the door flushed and out of breath. "You need to install an elevator. Those stairs are going to kill me," he panted.

"Where's the file?" I asked, choking back a laugh.

He handed it to me. I pulled out the photos and went through them in minute detail with a magnifying glass.

"Damn it! How could I have missed that?" I admonished myself.

"Missed what? Just what in the hell are you talking about?" he asked.

"I need you to get a crime lab team to Madame Phoebe's store now. I want them to perform a flourescein reagent test," I said.

He pulled his cell phone out of his coat pocket and dialed. "They'll be there in ten minutes," he said.

"Great, let's go," I said, struggling into my coat, my arm still sore from the gunshot wound.

"What exactly are we looking for?" he asked, helping me into my coat.

"Don't you find it odd that the only footprints we found were on the tablecloth, yet no blood was found outside of the backroom? There's only one way in and out of that store, and that's through the front door. There should have been blood tracked through the store on their shoes, especially given the way the place was ransacked. I just can't believe I missed that!" I exclaimed.

"Don't be so hard on yourself. We all missed it. Plus, Madame Phoebe was a friend of yours, you were upset," he said.

"That's no excuse. I still should have caught it," I sighed.

We arrived at Madame Phoebe's store to find the crime scene unit unpacking their gear. Detective Wilder unlocked the door and I walked in ahead of him to turn on the lights. The crime scene personnel followed us in and began setting up their equipment.

A flourescein regent test requires that two solutions be sprayed on all surfaces. Once completed, UV light is then used to detect any blood, even blood scrubbed away by cleaners. Any blood present will react to the light and glow.

Starting at the front door and working their way back to the rear of the store, several technicians fanned out and began spraying the first solution on every available surface, retracing their steps with a second solution. The lights of the store were turned off shrouding us all in darkness. Then, using hand-held UV lights, they began to search for any sign of blood. Detective Wilder and I peered out of the doorway of the back room anxiously waiting. After a few minutes one of the technicians yelled that he found something. He extracted an orange evidence marker out of his waist pouch and set it in place. By the time the technicians finished, a clear pattern of footprints emerged. Three sets of footprints lay clearly illuminated in a path from the backroom of the store to the front door. One set showed the hiking boot, another the dress shoes, and the third set revealed a high-heeled boot. Various other prints showed up in a more scattered pattern as the killers performed their frantic search for the skull.

"Amy Conterri was here at the time of the murder!" I exclaimed.

"You're sure?" he asked.

"Pretty sure. The night Madame Phoebe was murdered, Amy showed up at my house. She was wearing high-heeled black boots. I think the hiking boot belongs to Scott Jacobs," I said.

"And the dress shoe? To DePaulo's other henchman?" Detective Wilder said.

"I don't know. Maybe," I said, shaking my head.

"I'm going to get another search warrant for DePaulo's suite and Amy Conterri's house. We'll nab the shoes and test them in the lab. If we come up with a match, I'll take it to the district attorney to issue arrest warrants. Until the tests come back, I have them all under surveillance," he said.

"Good. Let me know what you turn up. I'm going to work on finding that murder weapon," I sighed.

"Okay. Take care, Savannah," he answered, letting me out of the store and locking the door behind me.

I drove back to the office and found Michael waiting for me. We spent a couple hours going over the renovation plans and estimate he'd gotten from the contractor, as well as choosing carpet, selecting the stain color for the built-in bookshelves that were going to be installed in the library. We also looked through several catalogs selecting furniture for Michael's office, the conference room, and the library. Before heading home for dinner, I wrote a deposit check for Michael to give to the contractor. Work would begin the following week.

After dinner, I locked myself in the den to think. There were very few places the murder weapon could be, and we'd already eliminated most of them. As careful as the killer was, I highly doubted he would just throw it in the trash somewhere, or dispose of it in some other careless manner. No, it was securely tucked away somewhere. I just had to find it.

I sat up most of the night waiting for a call from Detective Wilder, but it never came. Finally, around two in the morning, I took a pain pill and went to bed.

Chapter Twenty-Three

The alarm started blaring at six. I got up at seven, only because the aroma of fresh coffee and frying bacon lured me out of bed.

I wandered into the kitchen, poured a cup of coffee, and took a seat at the table. Lilly stood at the stove in her pink robe and fuzzy bunny slippers cooking bacon and eggs.

"Lilly," I said. "If you were going to hide a murder weapon, say a gun for instance, where would you put it?"

Lilly paused for a moment holding the spatula like a baton in mid-air.

"Well, I've always heard that the best place to hide something is in plain sight. So, I think that's where I'd put it," she answered, dishing up breakfast.

"Hmmmm. Interesting. I hadn't thought of that. Thanks, Lilly," I said.

"Anytime, Dear," she smiled, flipping on the television to watch the morning news while having breakfast.

Knowing better than to interrupt her morning show, I quickly ate my breakfast and got ready to leave.

I got to the office and spent an hour or two going through my mail and thinking about where the gun could be. Jackson called and suggested lunch at the Fisherman's Grill. I readily agreed. We'd spent very little time together lately and I missed him.

At noon I met Jackson outside the police station and we walked through town to the restaurant. Being lunch hour, we had to wait a couple minutes for a table.

After ordering, Jackson and I spent a few minutes catching up on each other's lives. Just as our lunch arrived, two older women sat down at the table next to us.

"Such a shame about, Mabel," a woman wearing a gray dress said.

"Yes, it is. But they did a good job on her," the other woman agreed.

"They did. And wasn't it nice of Mabel's daughter to put a picture of our card club in the casket with her," the woman in the gray dress said.

"Oh my God. That's it!" I exclaimed.

"What's it? What are you talking about?" Jackson asked.

"I have to go! I just had an epiphany," I said, slipping my arms into my coat.

"An epiphany? Don't they have pills for that now?" he teased.

"Oh, shut up, Jackson," I laughed, scrambling to my feet.

On my way out I stopped and put my hands on the shoulders of the woman in the gray dress. "You are the most amazing woman! Thank you!" I exclaimed, kissing the startled woman on the cheek before darting out of the restaurant.

I ran through town and arrived breathless at the funeral home in less than three minutes.

"Can I help you?" an older man in a black suit asked.

"Yes," I said, gasping for breath. "Do you have surveillance equipment in the viewing parlors?"

"We have video cameras, if that's what you mean," he replied, puzzled.

"Great. I need the video tape for the day of Phoebe Conterri's funeral," I said.

"Those tapes are for security reasons only. They are not available for public viewing," he replied stiffly.

"I can appreciate that. My name's Savannah Williams, and I'm working with the police on Phoebe Conterri's murder. I have reason to believe that the killer attended her funeral and I need to see that tape," I said firmly.

"I'm sorry, Ms. Williams, but I can't release that tape without proper authorization," he said.

"No problem," I replied, grabbing my cell phone out of my bag and dialing Detective Wilder's cell phone number. After explaining my theory to Detective Wilder, he agreed to come to the funeral home.

Upon his arrival at the funeral home, and a short conversation with the owner, we were given the tape. We met at my office to view it.

Watching the tape it became quite evident that its only purpose was to ensure that no one tampered with the body. The camera must be mounted above the casket, because the only view was of Madame Phoebe lying in her coffin and the first row of seats. Whenever someone approached the casket, all that could be seen is their hands and forearms.

We watched as several hands tucked crystals, crosses, and other talismans into the coffin with Phoebe. Then, we saw a pair of man's hands reach into the casket and tuck something wrapped in a white cloth under her body near her thighs.

"There it is," I whispered, stopping the tape.

"I think you're right. Rewind it," Detective Wilder said.

We rewound and replayed the tape several times trying to see what the man put in the casket, but couldn't make it out.

"Do we have enough for a court order to get her body exhumed?" I asked.

"We should. Let me take the tape. I'll call you when I know anything. We got the shoes from Amy Conterri's and DePaulo's. We should know something today. They were none too happy about it, that's for sure," he said.

"I can imagine," I chuckled.

"They can't sneeze without me knowing it," he assured me.

"Good. Call me," I said.

"I will. Talk to you soon," he said and left.

An hour later he called. "Everything's set. The body will be exhumed at four. Meet me at the cemetery."

"Wouldn't miss it for the world. See you then."

The rest of the afternoon seemed to go at a snails pace. Finally, at three-thirty I left the office and made the short drive to Oakdale Cemetery.

I arrived at the same time as Detective Wilder, an evidence technician, and the cemetery workers. The funeral director arrived a few minutes later with the key to the casket.

We watched in solemn silence as the backhoe dug into the soft earth finally revealing the top of the burial vault. A few minutes later, the backhoe driver raised the casket and set it gently on the ground.

"Open it," Detective Wilder ordered Mr. Edwards, the owner of the funeral home.

Reluctantly, Mr. Edwards inserted the key into a small hole near the head of the coffin. I heard a decisive click as the lock released the lid.

Unable to look, I turned my back to the scene. Dead bodies have always made me squeamish.

"Good job, Savannah. We got it," Detective Wilder said.

Turning around, careful to avoid looking at Madame Phoebe's body, I saw the evidence technician holding a large plastic bag containing a small bundle wrapped in a white cloth. Using a pair of long tweezers, he reached inside the bag and carefully pulled back the edges of the cloth revealing a mean looking gun. All of us stood there in stunned silence. Finally Mr. Edwards spoke up.

"How crass," he said.

We all nodded in agreement.

"Okay, let's pack it up and get out of here. We've got a lot of work to do," Detective Wilder said.

Mr. Edwards resealed the coffin and the workman began the process of laying Madame Phoebe to rest once again.

The evidence technician sealed the evidence bag and began to pack up his equipment.

"You going to be okay?" Detective Wilder asked.

"I'll be fine. Sorry. You go test the gun. I'll be at my office," I answered.

"Okay. Call me if you need me," he said, heading over to his truck.

"I will. Talk to you later," I said, waving.

I drove into town and returned to the cemetery a little while later with a bouquet of flowers. The cemetery workers were just finishing up and I waited in the warmth of my truck until they'd loaded up their equipment and headed out of the cemetery.

I walked over to Phoebe's grave and lay the flowers gently on top of the fresh mound of dirt.

"I'm so sorry, Phoebe. This should never have happened. Why didn't you call me?" I sobbed, tears running down my face.

Two hands gripped my shoulders and gently turned me around. I found myself face to face with DePaulo. Wordlessly he pulled me into his arms and I burst into tears.

"Shhhh," he whispered, stroking my hair. "It's okay."

After a few minutes I pulled myself together and wrestled out of his arms. "I'm sorry. I hate falling apart like that. What are you doing here anyway?" I said, wiping away my tears with the back of my gloved hand.

"Looking for you. I saw you at the flower shop and followed you. I'd like to talk to you some more. May I take you to dinner?" he asked.

"I really don't think..." I began.

"You really don't think what? That it's appropriate for you to be seen with such an unscrupulous rogue such as myself? Or that you shouldn't be seen with one of the main murder suspects in the death of your friend?" he asked, his eyes twinkling in amusement.

"No, it's not that," I stammered. "It's just that I have a boyfriend and his mother is my housekeeper and it just gets complicated."

DePaulo's laughter echoed through the cemetery as I explained my domestic situation.

"Come. It's just dinner. Besides, can you honestly say you wouldn't enjoy making that boyfriend of yours just a little bit jealous?" he cajoled.

"You win!" I said, laughing. "Where do you want to meet?"

"Let's go to Poseidon's. I've found they have excellent European cuisine," he said.

"Poseidon's it is then. But first, can I ask a question? What size shoe do you wear?" I said.

"Eleven. Why?" he said, puzzled.

"Just curious," I answered with a sly smile. "I'll see you there in ten minutes."

DePaulo held out his arm for me to take and escorted me back to my truck. On the way to Poseidon's I called Lilly to tell her I wouldn't be home for dinner.

"Oh, okay. But Jackson's here and Sandra was supposed to be here a half hour ago," Lilly said.

"She's probably just stuck in traffic. Have you tried her cell phone?" I asked.

"No. Do you have the number?" Lilly asked.

"Yes," I said, and rattled off Sandra's cell phone number. "I'm sure she's just running a little late. Try not to worry. I'll see you in a couple hours."

"Working late?" Lilly asked.

"Something like that," I said, catching myself blushing slightly.

"Be careful. I'll see you in a while," Lilly said and hung up.

Arriving at Poseidon's, Depaulo and I were seated in a quiet booth in the back and we spent a few minutes mulling over the menu. I decided on salmon, and DePaulo concurred. After perusing the wine list DePaulo ordered a very good, but expensive bottle of wine.

"Everything okay, Ms. Williams?" he asked. "You seem a little distracted."

"No, everything's fine. My housekeeper is a little worried because my friend, Sandra, is late for dinner," I answered. "And please call me

Savannah. I cried on your shoulder for goodness sake!"

"As you wish. And you call me Viktor, yes?" he said.

"Actually, I prefer DePaulo, if you don't mind. It just sounds more exotic," I smiled.

"Ahh, the lady likes an air of mystery around her men. I shall remember that," he teased.

"On a more serious note, are you ever going to be completely honest with me about the skull and the diamond?" I asked.

"Yes. One day I shall, but not tonight. Tonight is for you to relax and catch your breath. We just enjoy each other's company this evening, yes?" he replied.

"Yes," I agreed, smiling at him over my wine glass.

The salmon arrived perfectly prepared and conversation over dinner remained lively and entertaining.

We ordered an after dinner drink and I lit up a cigarette and sat back in the booth satisfied and relaxed.

The ringing of my cell phone broke the mood and I fished it out of my bag.

"Savannah Williams," I answered.

"Hi, Savannah, its Detective Wilder. I've had arrest warrants issued for Scott Jacobs and Amy Conterri, I'm bringing them in. Officers are on the way to serve the warrants," he said.

"Excellent, but there's one more person involved in this whole mess," I answered.

"I know, and hopefully Amy Conterri or Scott Jacobs will spill their guts and tell me who it is. We lifted a good set of prints from the gun found in Phoebe Conterri's casket, but so far the computer hasn't made a match," Detective Wilder said.

"Keep me posted," I answered.

"Will do. Later," he said, hanging up.

"A break in the case?" DePaulo asked eagerly.

"Looks like it. Scott Jacobs and Amy Conterri are being arrested," I said.

"So its over?"

"Not yet, but close," I answered.

Before DePaulo could respond, my cell phone rang again.

"Savannah Williams."

"Bring the diamond to Madame Phoebe's grave in thirty minutes. Come alone or your friend Sandra dies," a man's voice said. I could hear Sandra's cries in the background right before the line went dead.

I felt the color drain out of my face as the phone slipped from my hand onto the seat of the booth.

"Savannah! What's wrong?" DePaulo asked concerned.

"I have to go. The killer has Sandra!" I exclaimed, quickly gathering my things and rushing from the restaurant.

Breaking every driving law in the book I arrived at my office in record time. My hands were shaking as I dialed the combination to my safe. After three tries I finally got it open and withdrew the pouch with the crystal in it that I'd taken from Madame Phoebe's store. With the banks closed and no way to get the real diamond, I prayed fervently that the fake diamond would fool the killer in the darkness of the cemetery.

"Once Sandra is safe, I'm gonna kill him," I swore, slamming a fresh clip into my gun.

I tucked the gun in my jacket pocket and strapped a smaller, but equally as powerful weapon to my right ankle. I placed the pouch in the left pocket of my coat. After pulling my hair back into a ponytail to keep the wind from blowing it into my eyes, I was ready.

On the way I tried to figure out who made the call. Whoever it was must have used some type of device to disguise his voice.

Extinguishing my headlights, I cautiously drove through the entrance to the cemetery and parked. Everything appeared quiet. Hazy clouds hung in the sky effectively filtering most of the moonlight. An amorphous fog from the nearby lake threaded its way among the gravestones like wraiths performing a macabre dance. The air felt thick and oppressive, and I found it hard to breathe.

"Sandra is depending on you, Savannah. Calm down," I said to myself, taking a few deep breaths.

Using the larger tombstones and gnarled old oak trees for cover, I began to make my way slowly towards Madame Phoebe's grave lying near the back of the cemetery. Pausing every few feet to listen for the sound of voices or movement, I could hear Sandra's muffled cries from somewhere in the darkness.

As I moved closer and closer to Phoebe's grave I scolded myself for not calling Detective Wilder and requesting back up.

"Then again," I thought, reaching into my pocket and releasing the safety on my gun. "Murder should never have a witness."

Chapter Twenty-Four

Peeking out from behind a large monument, I saw a man and Sandra standing next to a tree by Phoebe's grave. I couldn't make out the man's face, but I recognized Sandra by her sobs.

"Let Sandra go and I'll give you the diamond," I yelled from my hiding place.

"Savannah!" Sandra wailed.

"Quiet, Sandra. It's going to be all right," I assured her.

"Come out where I can see you," the man yelled.

Steeling myself, I stepped out from behind the monument and into the open. I kept both hands in my coat pockets. One wrapped around the pouch, the other wrapped around my gun.

I saw the man had his forearm wrapped around Sandra's throat and a pistol pointed at her head.

"Throw out your gun," the man ordered.

Obediently I withdrew my gun from my pocket and tossed it next to a headstone a few feet away from me.

"Let Sandra go. This is between you and me," I called to the man.

"Show me the diamond," he ordered.

I pulled the pouch out of my pocket and emptied the crystal into my hand. Then held the crystal in my fingertips showing it to him.

"Okay, you toss me the diamond and I'll let Sandra go," he said.

"Let her go first," I answered.

"No deal," he said.

"Okay, how about this. I'll lay the diamond on top of this grave marker and walk over there,"

I said, pointing to a towering white monument about twenty feet away. "You let Sandra go and we all walk away from this thing."

"Do you honestly think I'm that stupid! My father thought I was stupid and look where that got him!" he raged.

"Paul Friedman," I whispered. Of course. It all made perfect sense now.

"Are you confessing to another murder, Paul?" I taunted him.

"It doesn't matter if I am. Neither one of you is getting out of here alive," he sneered.

Sandra started crying uncontrollably.

"Shut up, Sandra, or I'll kill you now," Paul said, jerking her neck back with his arm.

"Go ahead, Paul. Kill her. You'll be dead before she hits the ground," I said, inching my way toward my gun.

"Savannah!" Sandra pleaded.

"Stand still," Paul ordered, putting his finger on the trigger of the pistol.

"Okay, okay," I said, freezing in place.

"Now, toss the diamond at my feet," he ordered.

"Fine. Catch!" I yelled tossing the crystal high and long. "Sandra, duck!"

Dropping to the ground while reaching for my gun in the ankle holster, a shot rang out from somewhere behind me. I heard Sandra scream; then all went silent.

Quickly scrambling to my feet, I made a rolling dive for my gun lying on the ground. I sprung to my feet, gun pointed in front of me.

I saw Paul on the ground writhing in pain holding his right shoulder. Sandra was nowhere in sight.

"You can relax now, Savannah. Sandra is safe," DePaulo's voice said.

I turned and saw DePaulo walk out from behind a large tree. He had a small pistol in one hand and his other arm around Sandra who was crying softly.

"DePaulo?" I said.

"At your service," he smiled, taking a small bow. "Perhaps we should notify the authorities?"

"Right. Sandra, are you okay?" I asked.

Sandra nodded.

I walked over to Paul and kicked the pistol he'd been using well out of reach and pointed my gun at his head.

"Go ahead, pull the trigger," he taunted.

"Savannah, don't!" Sandra exclaimed, rushing to my side.

I heard the faint wail of police sirens in the background. DePaulo must have called the police.

"Savannah," DePaulo said. "Murder is so vulgar, so unrefined. You possess neither of those traits. Please, give me your gun."

"No!" I shrieked, tears gushing from my eyes.

Out of the corner of my eye I saw a steady stream of police cars and an ambulance wind their way through the cemetery toward us.

I turned my attention back to Paul. There were only seconds left.

"Savannah! Stop!" Jackson yelled from behind me.

Within what seemed like a split second, Jackson was standing next to me.

"Give me the gun, Savannah. He's not worth the trip," Jackson whispered, holding out his hand.

"But, Phoebe, he killed Phoebe," I cried.

"I know, Honey, but killing that scum won't bring her back," Jackson said.

Looking around I saw Sandra, DePaulo, Detective Wilder, and a slew of police officers around us. The lights from the police cars illuminated the scene. I saw Paul lying on the ground, his eyes filled with terror.

"You're right. Besides, there's too many witnesses," I said, easing my finger off the trigger and handing Jackson my gun.

Jackson put his arm around me and we headed out of the cemetery, stopping when we reached Sandra and DePaulo. Sandra and I hugged, holding each other tightly.

"You saved my life, Savannah," she said.

"No, DePaulo saved our lives," I answered, breaking our embrace.

"Thank you," I said, walking over to DePaulo.

"You're welcome," DePaulo said.

"Hey, wait. I thought you weren't prone to violence," I teased.

"Prone? No. Capable of it? Yes," DePaulo winked.

"Gotcha," I laughed.

"Why didn't you call me?" Detective Wilder demanded, rushing up to me.

"I forgot?" I said, shrugging my shoulders.

"Not likely," he retorted.

"How serious is Paul Friedman's gunshot wound?" I asked.

"Just a flesh wound. Paramedics are finished with him. He's well enough to answer a whole lot of questions, believe me," Detective Wilder answered.

"Good. I'll meet you at the station," I said.

"See you then," Detective Wilder answered. Paul Friedman walked by us in handcuffs escorted by a couple of burly looking police officers. I saw that his shirt was cut away and a large on his shoulder.

"Ms. Williams, did you forget something?" a police officer asked, holding out the crystal.

"Ahh, the diamond," DePaulo said.

"No, not the diamond," I said, taking the crystal from the policeman.

"Watch this, Paul," I said, placing the crystal on top of a flat headstone. I found a good size rock and brought it down hard on the crystal sending shards of glass everywhere.

Paul Friedman's eyes filled with rage.

"You honestly didn't think I would be stupid enough to bring the real diamond, did you?" I asked him, laughing wickedly.

"Get him out of here," Detective Wilder said. The officers lead Paul over to a waiting squad car.

"Jackson, take Sandra over to my house. Lilly must be worried sick. I'm going to the police station," I said.

"We're going to want a statement from her," Detective Wilder said.

"Can you have a detective get her statement at my house? She's been through a lot," I asked.

"No problem," Detective Wilder said, motioning to one of the detectives.

"See you later," Jackson said, giving me a kiss.

"Can't wait," I whispered.

I stood and watched everyone file out of the cemetery. DePaulo, noticing that I lagged behind, walked over to join me.

"You coming, Savannah?" he asked.

"In a minute, there's something I need to do first," I said.

"Would you like me to wait?" he offered gallantly.

"No. Thanks. I really need to be alone for a few minutes," I said.

"I understand," he said.

DePaulo put his arm around me and kissed my hair before disappearing into the darkness.

I walked over to Madame Phoebe's grave and sat down in the wet grass, and began arranging the dozen red roses I'd left earlier that day.

"It's over, Phoebe. You can rest now. Listen, you know I never much believed in all the paranormal stuff like you did. But, if you can, somehow let me know you're all right. I have Max. He's doing great and I promise to take good care of him, although I'm sure he misses you. I miss you too, Phoebe. I suppose I should thank you for the million dollars, but quite honestly I'm still at a loss as to why you did it, you know how I feel about blood money. I suppose I better get to the station. Detective Wilder will be waiting for me. Just know this, Phoebe. You are and always will be one of my best friends. I love you," I said, rising to my feet and brushing the dirt from my hands on my blue jeans.

I drove to the police station in Mt. Clements and Detective Wilder met me at the door.

"How's it going?" I asked.

"Good. We cut a deal with Scott Jacobs. Reduced the charge from murder one on Arthur Friedman to manslaughter. He's singing like a jay bird," he said, handing me the transcript from Scott Jacob's interrogation.

"Excellent. Is Amy Conterri talking?" I asked.

"Not a word. But it really doesn't matter. Scott's told us everything we need to know," he said.

"Can I see her?" I asked.

"Sure, she's in room three. Mind if I watch?" he asked.

"Not at all. In fact, you might enjoy the show," I laughed.

Detective Wilder and I walked up a flight of stairs and down a long hallway on the second floor.

"She's in there," he said, pointing to a room on the left.

I looked through the one-way glass and saw Amy Conterri sitting in a beat up wooden chair at a table. She looked dejected, but not scared.

"Hello, Ms. Conterri," I said, entering the room and standing across the table from her.

"Come to gloat?" she asked, still defiant in the face of certain defeat.

"Not at all. I just came to make my statement. Thought I'd pop in and say hi. I have to go now," I said turning to leave. "Oh, just one more thing. I wouldn't want you to spend the rest of your life in jail not knowing who the beneficiary is on Phoebe's life insurance policy."

"Who is it," she asked, leaning forward.

"Me," I said, smiling.

Amy leaped from her chair and came after me fast. I sidestepped her and allowed her forward momentum to carry her into the cinder block wall of the interrogation room, giving her a slight push. She hit it hard.

"Watch your step, Amy. We wouldn't want anyone to get hurt," I sneered. Laughing, I walked out of the room. Two police officers went in after me to put Amy back into her chair, handcuffing her to the table.

"You might want to watch her," I told Detective Wilder who witnessed the whole exchange. "She seems to be quite accident prone."

Detective Wilder chuckled as we walked to his office. I gave him a brief statement about what happened at the cemetery, promising to file my final report by the end of the week.

I walked out of the police station into the cold night air. I'd had to park a block away from the police station, so I slowly walked back to my Jeep. It'd been a long day.

Opening the door to my truck, I saw a red rose lying on my seat.

"What the hell?" I said, picking up the rose and placing it on the passenger seat.

Following a hunch, I stopped by the cemetery on the way home and walked over to Phoebe's grave. I counted the roses lying by her gravestone. There were eleven. I'd bought twelve.

"Thanks, Phoebe," I whispered.

Arriving home at midnight, I found Jackson, Lilly, and Sandra in the den waiting for me.

"Oh thank God you're all right," Lilly said, enveloping me in her arms.

"I'm fine, Lilly," I said, kissing her on the cheek.

"Wine?" Jackson asked, holding up a glass.

"Do you really have to ask!" I exclaimed, taking the glass and draining it in two gulps. Jackson thoughtfully poured me another.

"Sandra, you okay?" I asked, flopping down on the loveseat beside her.

"I will be. I still can't believe it was Paul. I loved him, Savannah," Sandra said, wiping a stray tear from her eye with a tissue.

"I know you did. I'm sorry it turned out this way," I said.

"You warned me and I didn't listen. And to think he almost destroyed our friendship!" Sandra said, shaking her head.

"It would take a lot more than a man to destroy our friendship, Sandra," I assured her.

"Okay! Now will you two stop gushing all over each other and tell me what happened?" Lilly demanded.

"Right. Well, it seems that Paul Friedman intercepted a call from Nancy Walker about the sale of the skull to the museum," I began. "Paul, knowing the diamond was concealed in the skull, began to formulate a plan. When Arthur Friedman took possession of the skull, he locked it in the safe in his office. Paul demanded to take the skull to an expert to have it appraised for insurance purposes, but his real plan was to take the skull apart and retrieve the diamond. Arthur Friedman flat out refused. Then Paul found out that his father was approached by DePaulo, who wanted to cut a deal to split the money from the sale of the diamond they both knew was hidden inside it."

"But, how did DePaulo know Arthur had the skull?" Sandra asked.

"Because he always knew that Thomas Markley had stolen the other half of the Star of Angels diamond. When DePaulo hired Scott Jacobs, Scott told him about the skull he'd seen while working for Thomas Markley. DePaulo simply put two and two together. Anyway, after Paul found out that DePaulo was in the picture, he panicked. He knew that if his father cut a deal with DePaulo the diamond would be lost forever. Having DePaulo as the perfect fall guy, Paul arranged for his father to have a little accident. You see, Paul Friedman and Scott Jacobs had practically grown up together. Their families vacationed together every year. Paul got a hold of Scott and hired him to cut the brake lines on Arthur Friedman's car, never dreaming that his father would be killed. After Arthur Friedman's death, Amy Conterri approached Paul to cut a deal. Paul had no choice but to accept Amy's proposal. After all, if he didn't Amy could turn Paul in for the murder of his father.

Paul Friedman and Scott Jacobs staged the break-in at the museum. They were searching for the skull. That's when they found the letter Arthur Friedman had written to Phoebe.

So, Paul, Amy, and Scott all went to pay Phoebe a visit and get the skull, but Phoebe didn't have it. She'd mailed it to me that morning. Things got ugly, and Paul shot and killed Phoebe. Then the three of them dismantled the store trying to find the skull. After cleaning up the bloody footprints in the store, Paul and Scott left and Amy called the police to report she'd just found her sister murdered. The rest you know," I finished.

"So what happens now?" Lilly asked.

"All three of them are going down. Paul for conspiracy to commit murder for his father, and murder one for killing Madame Phoebe. Amy is being charged with attempted murder among other things. She's the one who shot me that day at the beach. Scott Jacobs cut a deal with the district attorney and is going to be charged with manslaughter for the death of Arthur Friedman," I said.

Lilly started to ask another question but was interrupted by the ringing of the doorbell.

I answered the door to find DePaulo standing on the porch. He'd still been at the station giving his statement when I'd left.

"Sorry about the lateness of the hour, may I come in?" he asked.

"Of course. We're in the den," I said, stepping aside allowing him to enter.

"Thanks for what you did tonight," Jackson said, rising to shake DePaulo's hand.

"You're welcome, but I only did what any other gentleman would do," DePaulo said.

"Would you care for a drink?" Lilly asked him.

"Please. Scotch, neat, if you have it," DePaulo answered.

Lilly scurried off to the kitchen to prepare DePaulo's drink.

We all sat around the den for another hour discussing the twisted set of facts that found us all thrust together.

Finally, DePaulo got up to leave.

"May I escort you home?" DePaulo asked Sandra.

"I'd like that. Thanks," Sandra said, obviously smitten.

"Are you sure you want to be alone tonight?" I asked Sandra.

"I won't be alone," Sandra answered with an evil grin.

"I will stay with her until she falls asleep," DePaulo said.

"I'm sure you will," I laughed.

DePaulo and Sandra left arm in arm a few minutes later.

"Well, I'm going to bed. I'm exhausted," Lilly announced with a yawn.

"Me too," I agreed, yawning back.

"Allow me to stay with you until you fall asleep," Jackson said, nuzzling my neck.

"I wouldn't have it any other way," I said, taking his hand and leading him into the bedroom.

Epilogue

The weeks and months that followed were interesting to say the least. After turning over the missing half of the Star of Angels diamond, a hearing was conducted in an international court. The court determined that DePaulo is the rightful owner of the diamond and returned it to him.

Paul Friedman, Amy Conterri, and Scott Jacobs were tried and convicted on all counts.

DePaulo sold the diamond and put some of the money in trust to ensure the future of the Museum of Natural History. He also became the new curator of the museum, much to Sandra's delight. DePaulo also set up the Phoebe Conterri Foundation, which provides grant money to parapsychologists or organizations to study paranormal phenomena. Phoebe would have loved that.

Since I was out of the office a lot testifying at the trials, Michael Clayton took on the responsibility of the office renovations and the backlog of cases that piled up during my investigation of Phoebe's death. I must say he did a remarkable job.

DePaulo gave me the crystal skull as a memento and I have it displayed in a custom-built case in my office. But it represents much more to me. Never in my life had I ever come so close to committing cold-blooded murder, and it scared me. The skull acts as a reminder of how close I came to crossing the line between right and wrong.

Needing time to sort things out, I left Lilly in charge of the house and the animals, Michael in charge of the business, and took a two-week vacation to Mexico. I visited the Mayan ruins where Rubin Fleming first discovered the skull, and spent a lot of time walking through the rain forest near the hotel.

I arrived home the week before Christmas and had to do a ton of shopping to get ready for the holiday. Jackson, Sandra, DePaulo, Lilly and I spent the holidays together. While I'd been away, DePaulo and Sandra began a flourishing friendship, and very romantic love affair. I couldn't be happier for Sandra. She deserves some happiness after what Paul put her through.

Lilly keeps pushing for Jackson and I to get married, but we talked about it, and neither one of us is ready for that kind of commitment. We want to take our time getting to know each other.

But truthfully, I don't think I even know myself.

336
471 Shane
1702

Pro
14:35